DANNY ORLIS MAKES THE TEAM

DANNY ORLIS MAKES THE TEAM

By

BERNARD PALMER

MOODY PRESS

CHICAGO

Printed in the United States of America

CONTENTS

Chapter 1

CLIFF ARRIVES ON THE "EMPRESS"

IT WAS A DARK, COLD DAY on the Lake of the Woods, and the hint of fall was in the air. Out on the bay long, deep-throated breakers were running, and now and then rain dimpled the rolling waters of Pine Creek.

Danny Orlis had slipped into his deerskin jacket and was busy changing the grease in his outboard motor before putting it away for the winter. Blackie, his pet crow, flew over to the prow of a nearby boat and began to shout at him.

"Go on, Blackie," Danny scolded. "Go away and mind your own business. I haven't got time to mess with you today."

It had been difficult going away to school the year before, but this time it seemed even worse. Now he knew how much he would miss the quiet beauty of the Lake of the Woods. He knew how much he would miss his folks and Blackie, and the fellows from the boats who stopped overnight at his home.

He knew how lonely he could get for the cry of a loon, and the thrill of being pulled over the snow by a dog-team. It was almost enough to make a fellow feel like he ought to quit school and go to work or something. But he knew that he couldn't do that.

Suddenly he heard the sound of a boat in the distance.

"Did you hear that, Laddie?" he asked the shepherd dog at his side. "It sounds like the 'Empress.' "

In a moment or two he could see the blunt prow of the sturdy little packet boat bouncing over the waves as she quartered into the white-laced breakers to enter the calm of the creek.

"It is the 'Empress,' Laddie!" the young woodsman cried, scrambling to his feet. "Come on. Let's see if Cliff's aboard!" He dropped his tools and ran out onto the dock.

A boy about Danny's own age, only taller and fairer stood on the foredeck of the "Empress" with the bowline coiled loosely in his hands. "Hi, Danny!" he called.

"Hi, Cliff! I was afraid you wouldn't make it!"

"I got Joe to do my chores. Catch!" Cliff tossed the line to Danny who caught it and snubbed the "Empress" to the dock. "Boy, was it ever rough coming across the Big Traverse today!" he exclaimed as he jumped nimbly onto the rough planks of the pier. "Thought I was really going to be sick before we got to Oak. My old stomach was going up and down and around and around."

Danny laughed. He and Cliff had been pals ever since Cliff had started working on the "Empress," one of the little boats that plied the Lake of the Woods, hauling freight, and mail, and passengers. The two boys helped Captain Sterling get the freight unloaded, then they walked off the dock and out toward the log cabin where they usually slept.

"Did you talk to your mother and dad?" Cliff asked eagerly.

Danny nodded. "I did this morning, but it doesn't look too good. They both seem to think that I ought to go back to school in Iron Mountain."

"Boy, that's rough," his companion sighed wearily.

"You can say that again."

"We were counting on you to come down to Warroad," Cliff went on. "Why, just last night the coach stopped and asked me to tell you that he certainly wants you in the backfield of our football team this fall."

Danny Orlis picked up his rod and put it over in the corner of the cabin. "That would really be swell," he said. "And besides, if I went to school in

Warroad I could get back home once in awhile."

"Why don't you talk to them again, Danny?" Cliff asked. "If they knew how badly we all want you to come to the Warroad school, they might change their minds."

Danny sat down on the edge of one of the bunk beds and cradled his chin in his hands.

"I'd certainly like to go to school in Warroad," he continued. "And if it weren't for Larry I think I'd do everything I could to try and talk the folks into letting me stay with you this winter and go to school."

"Larry?" Cliff echoed. "Who's he?"

"He's the one who took Christ as his Saviour just before he went to the reformatory," Danny explained. "He really meant it when he became a Christian, too. He's been witnessing to his buddies and everything. I guess he's even got a little Bible study or Sunday school class or something like that right there in the reformatory."

"Boy, that's something," Cliff agreed. "But if he's saved now why does it make any difference whether you're going to school there or not? He'll get along okay."

"It's going to be hard for him," Danny explained. "He wrote and told me that he just can't stand to think of going back to Iron Mountain and meeting all the people who know what happened to him. They know where he's been and what he used to be like before he became a Christian. He says that he knows he couldn't do it if he didn't have me to go to school with."

"I guess I don't blame him at that," Cliff replied after a time. "It would be tough to have to go back home and try to live a thing like that down."

"So I've just got to do what I can for him." Danny stopped shortly. "Say!" he exclaimed, "I'm getting an idea. Why don't we see if we can't get Larry to come up here and go to school with us? Nobody would know anything about what had happened, and he wouldn't have to worry about facing people or anything."

"That's a swell idea," Cliff replied.

It had started to rain outside, a cold driving rain that whipped over the water in the teeth of the wind.

"Did you hear that?" Danny asked.

Cliff listened a moment. "No, what?" he asked.

"I thought I heard a foghorn," he went on. "Did you see the 'Dauntless' today? She's due up here with the mail, you know."

"That's right," Cliff answered. "This is mail day. But we didn't see her when we came in."

The sound came again, long and low and mournful.

"That's the 'Dauntless.' Come on, Cliff."

The two boys slipped into their jackets and went running out to the dock.

"Captain Brown will never dare to bring her in without someone to lead him along the channel," Mr. Orlis was saying. "You'd better go out and meet her, Danny."

"Okay, Dad," he replied. "Want to come along, Cliff?"

"Sure thing," his pal answered.

Chapter 2

MAN OVERBOARD

DANNY ORLIS AND CLIFF MORRISON jumped into Danny's boat and headed out toward the sound of the foghorn. The stubby little boat labored valiantly through the waves and Danny huddled deeply into his jacket collar to keep out the rain. As they edged out into the mouth of the creek where the wind blasted them with all its fury, Danny's boat lifted and fell heavily with each successive wave.

"Do you see anything?" Cliff shouted above the wind.

"There she is!" Danny cried. "Just off the port bow!"

Danny turned toward the larger craft, angling into the waves. The boat rolled dangerously and shipped water.

"Watch it!" Cliff shouted, grasping both sides of the boat with his hands. "It's too cold to take a bath out here!"

"Just take it easy! I'm not going to spill you!"

Danny cut the speed even lower, so the boat

nosed over the waves and inched the bow around until they were headed directly toward the big boat. As they neared the "Dauntless," which was wallowing sluggishly in the big breakers, they could see men running excitedly across the upper deck.

Two men were trying to get into the water the snub-nosed plywood scow which the "Dauntless" carried on her deck, while someone else had a life preserver on a long line in his hand.

"Do you suppose she's sinking?" Cliff demanded tensely.

Danny's heart came up in his throat and stuck there. The "Dauntless" was lying in the trough of a big wave, rolling dangerously as she lifted to the crest, and quivered from bow to stern as the long sea slipped out from under her. The next wave clammed against her planking and set the spray showering across her upper deck, but she didn't seem to be riding any lower in the water than usual, and Captain Brown was still at the wheel.

As the boys drew nearer the mail boat, one of the men spotted them and shouted, "Man overboard! Man overboard!"

Danny felt his throat tighten, and his stomach squeeze up into a little hard knot. A man overboard in this storm!

"Where?" he shouted, shutting down his motor and cupping his hand to his mouth. "Where?"

The man in the big boat pointed beyond them, out into the dark, foam-laced water. Danny swung his small boat around. It was a dangerous thing to do in the high waves and with the "Dauntless" so very close, but every second counted. A man was out there in the water!

"You look for him, Cliff!" Danny ordered. "We'll go back and forth real slowly!"

Cliff Morrison had already slipped out of his shoes and, crouched in the bottom of the boat, was pulling off his trousers.

"Do you see anything?" Danny shouted.

"Not a thing!"

The man in the boat shouted to them and waved them farther out. The flat-bottomed skiff was in the water now, tossing helplessly over the waves like a cork as they tried to row.

"There!" Danny shouted. "I saw him, Cliff! I saw the top of his head!"

"Where? Where?" Cliff cried.

An instant later Danny's companion saw the person in the water come to the surface, fighting desperately. Danny saw him at the same time and whirled the boat about. Cliff jumped into the cold, wind-swept lake.

"Oh, heavenly Father," Danny prayed silently, excitedly, "help Cliff and whoever's out there in the water to get out of this safely."

With half a dozen long, powerful strokes Cliff reached the fellow in the water and grasped him firmly by the hair. An instant later one of the men in the skiff threw a life preserver to him and drew the two of them slowly toward the flat-bottomed boat.

Danny did not remember quite how Cliff and the fellow he saved were taken aboard the "Dauntless." He scarcely knew how he got aboard the big boat himself, but he did manage to guide his boat, the "Scappoose," up alongside the "Dauntless" and tie her fast.

"You did a good job, young fellow," one of the men exclaimed to Cliff who was lying there gasping for breath. His lips and cheeks were blue with cold and the goose pimples stood out on his arms and neck. "You did a mighty good job."

Somebody else brought a blanket and covered him.

"Is–is he going to be all right?" Cliff panted when he could speak. "Is he——" his voice trailed off expressively.

"We don't know yet. They're giving him artificial respiration now."

Danny stepped closer. The figure on the deck lay quite still. Danny looked at him closely, then straightened suddenly and sucked in his breath.

It was his cousin Larry! The boy who had just been in the reformatory! It was Larry from Iron Mountain!

Chapter 3

PRAYER BRINGS PAROLE

LARRY!" DANNY CRIED.

The boy on the deck groaned, and for a brief instant opened his eyes.

"He's alive!" Cliff breathed prayerfully, rolling over on his side to stare at the boy he had pulled from the water. "Thank God, he's alive!"

Larry coughed a little and the man giving artificial respiration looked up and smiled weakly, but he didn't stop; not even for an instant. The boy was coughing up some water now and the color was coming back into his cheeks.

"Yes, sir, son," one of the men behind Danny said, "your brother's mighty lucky these two chaps showed up just when they did."

"I know it," a familiar voice answered.

Danny whirled quickly to see Bob, Larry's older brother, standing there, his face white and his shoulders trembling.

"Bob," Danny exclaimed, "what are you doing here?"

"Didn't you get our letter?" his cousin asked. "We wrote and told you that we were coming."

"No," Danny told him. "We didn't even know that Larry was–was back home."

"He got back a week or so ago," Bob said softly, "but things were pretty tough for him at Iron Mountain. The folks thought maybe it would be good for him to get up here with you for a little while. You–you helped him so much before."

"But what happened?" Danny asked. "How did he happen to fall overboard?"

"I don't know," Bob answered. "He had been awfully sick crossing the big lake, and it was still terribly rough out here, but I didn't see him fall."

"He was standing in the back, sort of leaning over the iron railing," one of the passengers put in, "when a big wave hit us broadside and sent everything sprawling. It knocked him overboard. I happened to be looking right at him and saw it happen."

Danny sighed deeply. He knew how excitable and scared Larry could get. He was glad he had fallen overboard instead of jumping.

By the time Danny thought of Cliff again, his pal had fished his clothes out of the "Scappoose" and had dressed.

Captain Brown came up to them. "Do you think you could lead us in to the dock through the channel, Danny?" he asked. "We'll never make it if we don't get there before dark."

"Sure thing," Danny replied.

It had always seemed strange to him that Captain Brown, who had been on the lake for twenty years, still had to have someone to pilot him up Pine Creek to the Orlis dock.

When they got ashore the young woodsman's mother came bustling out and had them carry Larry into the bedroom and put him to bed.

"You'd better crawl into bed, too, Cliff," she said. "Look, you're turning blue, you're so cold."

"I–I'll be all right," Cliff chattered, "as soon as I get warm."

"Here," Mrs. Orlis said firmly, "you stand over by the fire. I'll make you some hot chocolate."

Danny went in and sat by Larry's bed for awhile, but his cousin didn't feel much like talking. He lay there with his eyes closed most of the time. The next morning, however, when Danny went in to see him, he was sitting up drinking a glass of warm milk.

"Hi, fella," the young woodsman said cheerily, "how do you feel now?"

"Hi, Danny," Larry replied, "I feel a lot better, I think. I'm warm anyway."

"We were coming out after you," Danny went

on, smiling. "You didn't need to try to swim to the dock."

"Believe me, I wouldn't have if I'd known how cold it was going to be," Larry laughed. Then the smile left his face. "I was never so surprised in my life, Danny. I'd been pretty sick and was leaning on the back railing when that big wave hit, and the first thing I knew I'd tumbled into the water."

"Cliff didn't fish you out a moment too soon," Danny said. "We thought surely you were a goner."

"Is Cliff the one who dove in after me?" his cousin asked. "Where is he? I'd like to thank him."

"The 'Empress' pulled out at half-past six this morning," the young woodsman replied. "But he'll be back tomorrow night."

Larry was silent for a long while. Then he said, "You know, Danny, I don't know how I can ever thank you for all that you've done for me."

"I haven't done very much," the young woodsman replied. "I haven't done nearly as much to help you as I'd like to do."

"If you hadn't led me to Christ before I had to go to the reformatory I don't know what I'd have done," Larry went on hesitantly, as though he hated to speak, but had to. "It was tough enough as it was, but I always knew that I had Someone to fall back on. You can't imagine what a help that was."

"Yes, I do," Danny said. "I have to call on Him all the time for strength and guidance."

"I certainly learned that God answers prayer," his cousin went on. "I didn't ask for a parole or anything because the guards and the rest of the fellows—almost everyone out there—said that I was just acting like a Christian so I'd get out quicker. I wanted them to know that I had really changed down in my heart. But, even though I didn't ask for it, the warden recommended me for a parole just as soon as I had served the minimum time."

"That's wonderful," Danny said.

His cousin finished his milk. "But it was back home that things were really bad," he continued. "Everywhere I went people stared at me, even in church and Sunday school. And most of the kids wouldn't have anything to do with me, even the guys who were my best friends."

"That's tough," Danny agreed.

"I just couldn't stand to stay there any longer," Larry continued. "Dad went to the judge and asked him if it would be all right for me to come up here and visit you for a short time."

"Boy, we were certainly glad to see you," Danny told him.

Mr. Orlis and Bob came in just then and they all went in to the kitchen for breakfast.

Chapter 4

AN IMPORTANT DECISION

FOR THE NEXT FEW DAYS Danny Orlis showed his cousins around the Angle country. He took them over on Harrison Creek where Manitoba and the United States meet. He showed them the site of the old Hudson Bay town and the Dawson trail that cut across country through the forests to Winnipeg. He took them over on the Canadian mainland in Ontario to show them an Indian muskrat camp where a Chippewa family lived during the trapping season, and up toward Penasse to Magnuson's Island, where old Fort St. Charles used to stand, and where now the old building has been restored and a beautiful altar erected to commemorate the lives of the first men who were massacred there.

Cliff Morrison came up and stayed over one trip, and they all went fishing and hunting for wild life so that Bob who made a hobby of photography could get some good pictures.

Every time they came upon an animal or bird

Bob would whisper to Danny, "Row us in just a little closer, I want him to show up larger on the picture. Can't you get us just a little closer to him?"

But Danny broke him of that one afternoon when they caught an old cow moose calmly feeding in the water. She didn't seem to know that they were around at all, so he kept rowing closer and closer. Bob snapped his picture and looked up to stare the startled moose squarely in the eye.

"Get us out of here!" he shouted. "Come on, Danny! Get us out of here!"

They all laughed that night as Danny and Larry told about it at the supper table.

"I was so busy taking the picture," Bob laughed with them, "that I didn't realize what I was seeing until all at once I looked up and there was that old moose not five feet from me. I wanted to get out of there fast!"

"Don't you ever say that you want me to get you closer to an animal again," Danny told him.

"Don't you worry about that. And if it's a moose I think I'll tell you to go the other way."

"You did take quite a chance, son," Mr. Orlis said presently. "You've got to be awfully careful about doing things like that."

That night as they were getting ready for bed Bob came over and sat down beside Danny. Larry was still in the house eating a sandwich.

"Larry certainly acts more like himself since we came up here," Bob began. "He acts more natural than I've seen him since–since his trouble."

"That's swell," Danny answered. "He does seem to be having a good time."

Bob took a small file from his pocket and began to clean his finger nails. "I almost wish he didn't have to go back to Iron Mountain. Everybody there seems to have it in for him. The guys' mothers don't want them to run around with him any more, and everyone treats him like he was a convict or something."

"Doesn't it make any difference that he's a Christian now?" Danny asked. "Don't they know that he's taken the Lord as his Saviour and is going to live a different sort of life?"

Bob looked at Danny queerly, not quite sure that he knew what he was talking about. Then he said, "And believe me, it's going to be tough for him when he goes to school, too. It'll be even worse than it is now."

" Maybe he could go to school up here at Warroad," the young woodsman suggested. "No one but Cliff and me would know what happened and we certainly wouldn't tell. He'd get along fine here."

"That sounds like a swell idea!" Bob exclaimed.

"I'm sure the folks would let him, too. They want to see him go some place where it will be a little easier for him to get hold of himself and live the way he ought to."

Larry came in just then. He grinned broadly when they told him what they had been talking about.

"Say, that would be something," he said. "And then we could spend our weekends up here on the Angle, hunting, and fishing, and trapping. Boy, that would be something!"

"We'll talk to Dad about it the first thing in the morning," Danny said, "to see what he thinks."

"This ought to solve a lot of things," Bob put in happily.

But the next morning Mr. Orlis was not too enthusiastic.

"I'm not going to tell you what to do, Larry," he said. "This is something that you will have to work out for yourself. But you've asked for my advice, so I can't do anything more than tell you what I think."

"That's what we want you to do," Larry answered.

"The easiest thing possible would be for you to come up here where nobody knows what has happened to you, and start over," Danny's dad began. "That would be simple and easy because you'd have a fresh start here."

"That's why we thought it would be a lot better," Danny put in.

"And," Mr. Orlis went on, "it would be hard to go back to Iron Mountain where everyone knows and probably looks down upon you. But the big question is this, what would God have you do? Would He want you to turn tail and run like a coward, or would He want you to stand on your own two feet and fight the thing out right there in Iron Mountain? Would He want you to take the easy way, or prove to those people back home that you're a Christian and a man?"

"Well," Larry stammered uncertainly.

"You think it over, Larry," Danny's dad concluded gently. "Don't make a decision right away."

"I have been thinking that I should testify to those fellows who were sort of mixed up with me in that radio club that got into trouble," Larry said, more to himself than to the others. "I was the leader. I really owe it to them to talk to them about Jesus, and to show them through my life what He has done for me. If I don't, the same thing might happen to some of them."

There was a long, unnatural silence. Then Danny said softly, "If you want to go back to Iron Mountain, Larry, I'll go with you and help you all I can."

Chapter 5

ORLIS THROWS A NICE PASS

DANNY AND HIS COUSINS, Bob and Larry, rode down to Warroad on the "Empress" the week before school was to start and took the bus to Fargo, crossing the Dakotas and Nebraska to Iron Mountain, Colorado. Cliff went down to the bus depot to see them off.

"You look after Blackie and Laddie for me, Cliff," Danny said as his two cousins climbed into the bus and sat down together.

"Sure thing," Cliff replied. "And if you go out for football, hit 'em a couple of times for me."

They both laughed a little.

"I certainly wish we were going to get to play together," Danny said reluctantly.

"Maybe next year."

The bus driver honked impatiently, and Danny said good-by to his pal and got aboard.

It was a long, tiresome trip out to Colorado and the boys were glad to get off the bus when they finally rolled into that little mountain community and stopped in front of the town's only hotel. Aunt Lydia was there to meet them and take them to their home.

"I'm so glad that you're back, Danny," she said, patting him affectionately on the shoulder. "We've been so terribly lonesome without you. I know you're going to be a big help to Larry."

"I'm glad to be back, too," the young woodsman told her. And, despite the fact that he was homesick already, he was glad to be back in Iron Mountain for school.

"You have no idea how your stay with us changed our family," she went on. "When you first came, we were so selfish and we didn't have time for God at all. Now your Uncle Claude and I go to church regularly." She paused a moment. "In fact, we both have found the Lord Jesus as our personal Saviour."

"That's swell," Danny answered, "that's really swell."

The next morning he and Larry went down to the little grocery store at the end of the block. The instant they entered, two women over in one corner stared at them intently, and then turned to one another and began to whisper. The storekeeper, who was stocking shelves, stopped working and watched every move that Larry made all the time he was in the store, just as though he expected him to pick up everything he could get his hands on and walk off with it.

"Did you see that?" his cousin asked almost sorrowfully when they were outside again. "Both of those women are in the church we go to now. I've been in Sunday school every Sunday since I—since I got back, and I've stayed for church too. But they still act like I'm a criminal."

Danny said nothing.

"I pray and pray and pray," Larry continued miserably, "but it gets harder to face people every single day."

It was the same way that first day of school as the two boys went together. Kids that Larry had known all his life turned to stare at him. And when he got into his division room and selected a desk, the two girls in front of him got their things together and moved.

"I don't think I can go back this afternoon," he said to Danny at noon as they stood on the steps of the building. "I just can't take it any more."

"I know how you feel," the young woodsman told him. "But you don't have to depend upon your own strength to take it. You've got the Lord Jesus to turn to. Let Him carry the burden."

"I know that," his cousin replied seriously. "And

if it weren't for Him, I know I couldn't possibly stick it out."

Both Larry and Danny checked out football suits that night after school.

"What position do you want to play, Danny?" the coach asked him.

"I don't care where I play," the young woodsman replied. "I just want to get a chance to play."

"That's the stuff," Coach Edwards said. "That's the way I like to hear a player talk."

The first few days they didn't do much of anything except calisthenics and running. But after about a week Mr. Edwards gave them a football and had them throwing and kicking. Danny hadn't had a football in his hands more than a half dozen times, but he had played a lot of baseball. He drew back and rifled the pigskin to Larry.

"You, Orlis!" the coach shouted. "Didn't anybody ever show you how to hold a football when you pass it?"

"No, sir," Danny replied.

"Well, here," the coach said, "you hold the ball in your hand like this."

The young woodsman grasped the pigskin carefully. "Is this right?" he asked.

The coach grunted. "And when you throw, bring your arm back over your shoulder the way Eric Tanner is doing."

Danny threw several passes while Coach Edwards stood there watching.

"You've got a good arm, Orlis," the coach said at last. "Keep working on those passes."

After practice Larry was jubilant.

"Boy, you're in, Danny," he said excitedly. "I heard Mr. Edwards tell one of the other coaches that you were a natural passer. He said, 'We're going to have a spot for that kid if we can just teach him the fundamentals.' "

Danny grinned. He didn't know much about football, that was sure. But he certainly would like to play.

The next afternoon, and the next and the next, the coach had the young woodsman throwing passes. One of the teachers who had played quite a little football in his high school and college years took Danny aside and worked painstakingly with him. He taught him how to hold the football, how to draw back his arm and throw so the ball could be easily caught by the receiver. He taught him how to fake and rifle a short, bullet pass just over the line. Danny threw until his arm and shoulder ached and still they called upon him to continue to throw.

"You throw a nice pass, Orlis," Coach Edwards said at last, calling Danny off to one side. "I'm going to build a few plays around you and figure on using you at left half, at least for a while."

"That sounds swell," Danny told him.

"In the meantime I want you to study hard on our plays," Mr. Edwards continued, "we may be calling on you to quarterback."

On Thursday night Larry and Danny went to Young Peoples.

"This is one bunch that won't turn on you," Danny said as they entered the church door. "I'm sure of that much."

"I—I hope you're right," Larry answered hesitantly.

Danny saw that strained, bewildered look come into his cousin's eyes as they entered the church, a frightened look like that of a young rabbit cornered against a pile of logs. But it only lasted momentarily. As he and Larry stepped into the doorway, the gang crowded about them. Danny saw a faint, relieved smile flicker on his cousin's lips.

Peggy Denton came up to him just then.

"Hi, Peggy," he said. "I'm glad to see you here." She was the girl he had been able to help lead to Christ the spring before.

"I won't be any place else on Thursday night," she replied.

"How are things going?" he asked her when they were able to be alone a few minutes later.

"I've got a lot of problems, Danny," she said. "Real problems. I'd certainly like to talk with you when you have the time."

"Sure thing," he said. "I'll see you after while."

Larry came up then, and Peggy moved away.

Danny wanted to get a chance to talk to Peggy and find out what she had been doing through the summer, but before the meeting started she was busy talking to some of the girls and as soon as it was over, she hurried out to meet Eric Tanner who was waiting for her just inside the front door.

Eric looked down at Larry who had just come out of the basement and was starting up the steps.

"Hi, Jailbird," he sneered. "What are you trying to do hanging around the church like this? Fool somebody into thinking you're a good little Christian?"

Larry's face blanched white.

Chapter 6

TROUBLE ON THE SQUAD

DANNY AND LARRY stood on the steps together as Peggy grasped Eric by the arm and swept him away. Larry's face had gone tense and white and his fists were knotting convulsively.

Danny looked over at him and saw the fierce anger in his cousin's eye. "Take it easy, Larry," he said softly. "Eric just does things like that because he knows he can get a rise out of you."

"I can't help it," Larry answered. "I feel so ashamed about what I've done that I can hardly stand to have someone rub it in like that all the time."

"I know how it must make you feel," the young woodsman went on as they walked home together. "But you want to be careful about losing your temper. You know the Lord expects us to be above that sort of thing. I know it's hard for you, but you want to put your trust in Christ to help you keep from getting mad."

"I—I'll try, Danny," his cousin answered doubtfully.

In the locker room on Friday evening before game time Eric came up to where Larry was standing.

"I told Peggy," the older boy said belligerently, "that she'd just as well stop trying to drag me down to that church of hers and make a Christian out of me. If they tolerate jailbirds, I'm not interested."

Larry's eyes flashed and his mouth drew down to a thin, hard line. He was biting his lips savagely for control.

"Lay off, Eric," Danny Orlis said quietly, getting to his feet. "Larry hasn't done anything to hurt you."

"You keep out of this," Eric snapped, turning toward the young woodsman. "You're probably a jailbird, too, if we just knew the truth about you. How does it come that you came halfway across the country to go to school? Are you hiding something?"

Before Danny could answer, Larry took a step or two forward. "You don't need to talk to Danny that way," he said. The team had crowded around by this time. "He hasn't done anything to be ashamed of."

Eric reached out to take hold of Larry's jersey

and Danny took a step toward them, but Coach Edwards appeared in the doorway just then.

"All right, you guys," he ordered, "out on the field. We've got a job to do."

"I'll see you after the game," Eric muttered under his breath. "And don't you forget it, either."

The game with Spring Creek was one-sided from the start.

Danny set up two touchdowns with his rifle passes over the line, and Eric Tanner scampered around end for a third. After that Coach Edwards shuttled his reserve strength in and out, giving them experience and trying out various combinations.

"A good game, fellows," the coach congratulated when the final whistle sounded. "Get home early now and get a good night's rest. We'll all be on deck Monday after school."

Danny and Larry were among the last in the locker room to get dressed. They started out of the room together, but Coach Edwards called to Danny.

"I'd like to talk with you for a couple of minutes, Orlis," he said. "You can go on ahead, Larry."

"Okay," Larry answered. "I'll wait for you outside, Danny."

When his cousin had gone, Danny went over to the bench and sat down across from the coach.

There was a long silence. Finally, Coach Edwards looked up.

"First of all, I've got to swear you to secrecy, Danny," he said. "You won't say anything to anyone about this, will you?"

Danny shook his head. "Not if you don't want me to."

"Not to anyone," the coach went on. "It's very important that no one except you and me know about this."

"I won't say anything," the young woodsman affirmed.

"Fine." The coach crossed his legs and, taking his pencil from his pocket, began to finger it absent-mindedly. "You seem to be levelheaded, and you're close to Larry. How is he doing?"

"Real well," Danny replied. "I'm proud of him."

"I'm glad to hear that," the coach went on. "You see, I've had two or three phone calls from mothers whose boys are playing on the team. They don't seem to like it because Larry's on the squad, too. They think he's a bad influence."

"He probably was a bad influence before," Danny said, "but just before he went to the reformatory he took Christ as his Saviour."

"Now what do you mean by that?" the coach broke in quickly.

"He did what the Bible tells us we should do,"

Danny went on. "He recognized that he had sinned and was headed for an eternity in Hell, and then he asked Jesus to cleanse him from sin. And he put his trust in Him for salvation. Ever since then Larry's been a different fellow."

Coach Edwards sat there for a long while.

"Larry does seem different at that," he said, more to himself than to Danny. "Well, as far as I'm concerned, those mothers can keep right on calling. He's going to keep on playing football."

When the coach finished talking, Danny hurried outside. If only he hadn't promised not to tell. This was something that would be a big help to his cousin, letting him know that someone had noticed the change in his life since he took Christ as his Saviour.

As Danny went out the side door of the school building, Larry came around the corner. His sweater was torn, the knee was torn out of his trousers, and one eye was already getting black.

"Larry!" Danny cried. "What happened to you?"

"Eric," Larry said numbly. "Eric and I got into a fight!"

"I guess you did."

"And what's worse, I've broken my parole!" He took a long breath. "They can send me back to the reformatory for this!"

Chapter 7

FACING THE CONSEQUENCES

DANNY TOOK ANOTHER CLOSE look at Larry's torn clothes and his puffed eye.

"How did it happen?" he asked.

"Eric was waiting for me just like he said he would be," Larry replied. "I—I came out of the door and there he was. He started calling me names and—and razzing me about where I had spent the summer until I couldn't take it any more and—and I swung at him. I don't know what happened after that. I hit him and he hit me. Then he knocked me down and ran away."

"That's tough," Danny said. He was thinking of what Coach Edwards had talked with him about. Those women who called the coach had been convinced that Larry wasn't a fit associate for their sons just because he had been sent to the reformatory. What would they say now?

"And the worst of it is," Larry went on bitterly, "I've broken my parole. If Judge Lambert ever finds out about this I—I'll be headed back to the reformatory for sure."

"He'll find out about it all right," Danny said. "In a town this size he'll hear about it soon enough. Maybe if we go and talk with him and tell him what happened, and how sorry you are about it, he'll give you another chance."

Larry sucked in his breath sharply. "I'd rather do most anything than go over and—and tell the judge about that fight," he said. "Do you really think I have to?"

"That's something you will have to decide," Danny told him. "But if it were I, I'd certainly go and see him just as soon as I could."

They went into the house and down to the basement to Danny's room.

"I suppose you're right," Larry said, sitting down wearily. "It seems as though I can't do anything right. I've been wanting to testify to Eric, too. Now I let something like this happen. What is he going to think of my testimony? What is he going to think of Jesus, when I acted just like anyone else would when he started to make fun of me?"

Danny was silent for almost a minute. "I think you've got something there," he said slowly. "If our testimony is going to mean anything to those who aren't Christians, then we've got to act differently from the way the world does."

Larry picked up the Testament from the table beside the bed. "If he had hit me first, it might not be quite so bad," he went on miserably, "but he didn't. I just got so mad I didn't know what I was doing and belted him one."

"It's too late to change that now," Danny told him. "It's already happened. The question is, what can we do about it?"

Larry rubbed his swollen eye tenderly. "Would—would you go over to Eric's with me in the morning when I go to apologize?"

"Why certainly, Larry," the young woodsman replied, smiling warmly.

"And then I'm going down to tell Judge Lambert all about it," he concluded.

Danny took a pencil from his pocket and began to finger it. "You know, Larry," he said. "Dad always tells me that we can't apologize or say we're sorry that we've done something just so we can get out of being punished for it. You—you aren't going over to apologize to Eric just so you can tell Judge Lambert that you've talked with him, are you?"

Larry shook his head. "No, Danny," he said fervently, "I want to apologize w-w-whether they send me back to the reformatory or not."

The next morning right after breakfast Danny

and Larry went over to Eric's house. The older boy was just getting dressed.

"Now what do you want?" he demanded sullenly when he saw the two of them standing at the door. He was barefooted and was just buttoning his shirt.

"I–I just wanted to talk to you a minute," Larry stammered, "about what happened yesterday afternoon."

"I don't know that I want to talk to you," Eric retorted angrily. "I taught you a lesson for not being able to take a little ribbing. What more do you want?"

"I–I'm sorry for starting the fight," Larry managed, forcing out the words. "Like you said, I–I should have been able to take a little razzing. It isn't Christian to do what I did yesterday, and I want to ask your forgiveness."

"You should have thought of that last night," Eric retorted, "before you hit me in the mouth and broke off that sixty-dollar artificial tooth of mine."

For the first time Danny noticed that one of Eric's upper teeth was gone, and he saw, too, the swelling and red line on Eric's lip where Larry's blow had landed.

"Did I break your tooth?" Larry asked.

"I certainly didn't do it myself," the taller, heavier boy said. "Why else do you think I tore into you?"

"I—I'm awfully sorry," Danny's cousin went on. "I'll stop down to see the dentist and see if I can't make some kind of arrangements to—to pay for it."

"*You* pay for it?" Eric snorted. "What would you do, go out and rob a filling station?" With that he slammed the door angrily.

Larry and Danny stood there looking at one another. Larry ran his fingers through his tousled hair. His face was pale and his lower lip trembled.

"He—he wouldn't even accept my apology," Larry said. "He wouldn't listen to me say that I was sorry for what I had done."

"You did your part," Danny told him. "That's the important thing."

On the way downtown to talk to Judge Lambert Larry stopped in at the dentist's office to see about getting Eric's tooth fixed.

"Why, he's already made arrangements for that," the dentist said. "We've had a temporary tooth in the cavity for the past two or three years to let his mouth grow. Now we're making a permanent tooth. I took out the other one yesterday afternoon and made an impression for the new one."

Larry looked over at his companion. "I—I can't understand it," he said. "Why do you suppose he would tell me that?"

Danny said nothing.

Judge Lambert didn't seem surprised to see them when they entered his big office in the courthouse. He didn't seem surprised, either, when Larry told him about the fight.

"You know that you broke your parole, don't you?" he asked, his eyes serious.

Chapter 8

AN UNEQUAL YOKE

FOR A MOMENT OR TWO Larry stood there, stark fear in his eyes. He blinked and swallowed hard.

"You know that you broke your parole," Judge Lambert repeated, "don't you, Larry?"

"Yes—yes, sir." He rolled his cap into a tight little knot. "I know I shouldn't have done it; I didn't have any excuse, but I am sorry that I did. And—and it won't happen again."

The judge got up and came around to the other side of his desk. "I'm glad you came to talk to me about it, Larry," he said. "It shows that you are trying to do what is right, and that you appreciate being paroled." He picked up a big sheaf of papers and began to thumb through them. "I've already had a report on your fight. If you hadn't come in voluntarily, I don't know what my decision would have been, but I'm willing to go along with you this time, Larry. Just don't let it happen again."

"Oh, thank you, Judge," he said, sighing deeply. "You won't need to worry. I surely won't be getting into any more fights."

Once outside the judge's office Larry sighed again. "You know," he said, "sometimes the hardest thing to do is to go right to the bottom of a thing like this and get it settled, but it surely is the easiest in the long run."

"That's right," Danny replied. "We can't run away from trouble. The easiest and best thing is to stand right up to it."

They crossed the street and started back home.

"You know, Larry," Danny said suddenly. "There's only one thing about this whole affair that you haven't taken care of."

"What's that?" Larry asked quickly.

"It's probably the most important thing, too," Danny went on. "You know, when we do something like this, we sin against God as well as against man. We ought to always confess our sin to God and ask His forgiveness."

"I've already done that," Larry answered, his face serious. "I did that the first thing, just as soon as I left you in your room last night. I went upstairs and prayed that God would forgive me, too."

The next week at school Eric glared at Danny and Larry when he met them in the halls. And on the football field he spoke to them only when he absolutely had to.

It had been clear from the very beginning of the football season, even from the opening practice, that Iron Mountain was going to have a strong team. Most of their linemen were seniors, and three of the backfield, including Danny, could run the hundred in ten seconds flat. They mowed down the first three teams they met without uncorking half of their best plays, or even using the regulars for more than two full quarters.

"I'm going to tell you fellows something," the coach said the evening after they beat Bordon handily for the fourth win in a row. "We've got the best possibilities for an undefeated season and the conference championship that we have ever had, if we all pull together. I'm going to insist that you fellows keep regular hours, keep your grades up, and give the very best you've got for every game. If you don't, I'm going to pull you out and put in somebody else." He paused a moment. "Tanner, here, is one who is apt to be benched. And so is Gustafson and Miller."

As they filed out of the locker room, Danny heard Gustafson say to Eric, "Do you think that he'd dare bench us?"

"Who's he got to put in my place excepting that skinny little jailbird, Larry?" Eric asked.

At the next regular meeting of the Young Peoples Peggy Denton came over to where Danny was sitting.

"Danny," she said seriously, "could I talk to you for a few minutes?"

"Sit down."

"Let's go some place where we won't be interrupted," she told him.

Together they made their way up the back stairs to the pastor's study.

Peggy sat down in the chair behind the big desk and Danny sat on the corner of the bench along the wall.

"I suppose it seems silly for me to come to you for advice when you're so much younger than I am," she began, twisting her handkerchief nervously, "but I've got to have someone to talk to." She took a deep breath. "I just don't know what to do."

"What seems to be the trouble?" he asked.

"It's Eric." She stopped and gulped hard. "I've talked with him and prayed for him and everything, but it just doesn't seem to do any good. The harder I try, the more stubborn he gets."

"Some people are like that, my dad says," Danny replied. "The more they hear the Gospel, the more they harden their hearts so it can't touch them."

"I just don't know what to do." She stopped again, and for an instant Danny thought she was going to cry.

"Did you hear the sermon Pastor Jones preached last Sunday?" Danny asked her at last.

She nodded silently.

"He said that we shouldn't be unequally yoked together, that Christian fellows shouldn't go with unsaved girls, and that Christian girls shouldn't go with unsaved fellows."

There was a long silence.

"Don't you remember how he pointed out that so many Christians ruin their lives and their testimonies by going with non-Christians and marrying them?" Danny went on. "Come to think of it, I believe I could name quite a few of them myself."

"I know," she said dully. "But I–I think so much of Eric. It's different with him. I just know it is. He's a good kid at heart. If I could just win him for the Lord!"

"That," Danny answered softly, "is the big problem."

"Would you pray for us?" she asked.

"Of course I will."

Chapter 9

AN OFFER IS MADE

DURING THE WEEK Coach Edwards worked the squad hard, sending the regulars through one scrimmage after another.

"This Creek outfit is tough," he said during a skull session on Thursday night. "They won the Conference championship two years in a row, and have got a good, solid team this year. We're going to have to get in there and fight every minute, or we'll be coming off the loser for the first time this year."

"The same old stuff," Eric snorted under his breath. "Do or die for dear old Iron Mountain."

He thought he was talking low enough so that only the fellow next to him could hear, but at that very moment the room quieted and everyone heard him.

For an instant or two Coach Edwards stood there, staring at Eric while the other fellows sat breathless.

"Tanner," he snapped at last.

"Y-y-yes sir," Eric Tanner stammered.

"For the past two weeks I've been warning you about not hustling out on the field," the coach lashed. "You're going to ride the bench tomorrow night. In fact, you'll sit in the stands. We aren't going to have room on our team for anyone with an attitude like that. And that goes for every one of you. If anybody else feels like Eric does, speak up. We might just as well know it now."

Nobody moved or spoke.

When skull practice was over Coach Edwards called Larry in and told him that he would be starting in Eric's place the following night.

"You're a little shrimp for an end," he said, grinning, "but I like your spirit. The way you've come back here and fought to earn the respect of everyone is something to be proud of. I wish I had a whole squad like you."

"It isn't I, Coach Edwards," Larry said modestly. "If I hadn't taken Christ as my Saviour, I'd have been sunk a long time ago. But with Jesus to help I've been able to keep working at it."

The coach picked up his pencil, stared at it thoughtfully, then laid it back on the desk.

"Well," he answered. "if being a Christian will make a fellow get in there and give all he's got like you and Danny Orlis do, then I wish every one of my squad would go for it."

Larry was almost in a dream as he and Danny walked home from practice and threw open the front door. To think that he was going to get to start, for this game at least, at end. He was on the first team!

"Guess what," he announced proudly as he walked into the room where the family was sitting. "I'm going to start in the game tomorrow night."

"You are?" Bob exclaimed. "What happened to Eric Tanner?"

"Nothing."

"Is he down in some subjects or something?" Bob persisted.

"Nope," Larry replied, grinning broadly. "Coach Edwards just told him that he didn't hustle enough so he's going to let him sit out one."

"I sure wish the coach had picked a different game for that," Bob said, looking at his younger brother disdainfully. "We're going to need every good man we've got to win this one."

"Don't you worry about Larry," Danny said loyally. "He'll take care of himself at end, all right."

"I surely hope so," Bob replied. "I'd hate like everything to have my brother responsible for Iron Mountain getting beat for the first time this year."

But Bob did not have to worry. Larry did take

care of himself all right at end. In fact, he played a topnotch game. He and Danny had practiced passing so much that he could snake the young woodsman's passes out of the air from almost any position, and he was fast and wiry enough to wriggle through the opposing line on almost every play.

The first time Iron Mountain had the ball the quarterback called for a short pass out into the flat.

"Number 53," he said, wiping the sweat from his hands. "Can you catch it, Larry?"

"I can sure try," the little end replied.

Danny took the pass from center, tucked the ball under his arm as though he were going to run with it, then dropped back and to the right, and rifled a feather-light pass to Larry, who was cutting in behind the defensive back diagonally across the field. He snatched the ball out of the air and scampered 28 yards before Valley finally forced him out of bounds. On the next down they repeated the same play to set up a touchdown on the Valley three-yard line. A roar of approval went up from the stands.

At the end of the game every bone and muscle in Larry's wiry little body ached, but there was no doubt as to who the hero of the game was.

"Boy, wasn't that something?" he asked excitedly as he and Danny started home after they had had a shower and dressed.

"You sure weren't missing many passes out there tonight," Danny told him. "I've never seen you like that before."

"You know," Larry said, "I prayed just about all night that God would help me in this game, not especially to win, but to do the very best that I possibly could."

Just then a long low convertible drove up alongside of them and stopped.

"Larry!" a fellow in the car called. "Come here a minute. I want to talk with you–in private."

"Okay," Larry said.

"I'll wait on the library steps," Danny told him.

The fellows in the car were talking in low tones and Danny's cousin was shaking his head emphatically. Once or twice he started to leave, but they called him back. Finally, however, one of the men said, "Think it over, Larry. We'll be seeing you." Then with the grating of gears the car sped away.

Larry came over to where Danny was sitting, his face an ashen white.

"What's the matter?" Danny asked. "What's wrong?"

"That was Woody Blackburn," Larry said softly, reluctantly. "He was in the reformatory when I was. He just got out a month or so ago."

"What did he want?"

For a long while Larry was quiet. Then he said, "They tried to make me promise not to tell, but I didn't. Woody, and that older fellow who was with him, have doped out a scheme to mop up the money by betting against Iron Mountain when we play Spring Creek. And—and they tried to get me to agree to throw the game."

Danny whistled in amazement.

"Say," he exclaimed. "We'd better tell Coach Edwards right away!"

Chapter 10

SOME THINGS YOU CAN'T DO

PEGGY DENTON, who had gone to the football game with Eric, was sitting with him in his old coupe in front of the drive-in when the contest was over.

"I've got a good notion to turn in my suit," Eric stormed, tearing open a package of cigarettes. "The idea of putting a skinny little jailbird like Larry in at end in my place. When it comes to that, I'd just as well quit."

"He surely caught a lot of passes," Peggy answered defensively.

"That was Orlis," Eric retorted, his voice rising. "If he'd throw like that to me I'd catch a lot of passes, too, but he doesn't. They come at me like bullets, and are just about as easy to handle. The two of them are working together to beat me out of my spot in the lineup. That's what they're trying to do."

"I don't think Danny would do a thing like that," Peggy replied, "nor Larry either. They're both Christians. They wouldn't try to take advantage of you."

"Don't try to kid me," Eric told her. "Just because they both pass out the same sort of religious stuff as you do is no sign they wouldn't knife me in the back if they could."

"Let's not quarrel about them, Eric," Peggy said softly.

"That's more like it." Eric reached over and turned on the radio. A swing band was playing. "Say now," he said, "that's some swell music, isn't it?"

"I guess it is if you like it," Peggy told him.

"Remember how much fun we used to have dancing to music like that before you went silly over religion?" he asked her.

"I remember that I used to enjoy it," Peggy said, coloring delicately. "But that was because I didn't know any better. It—it seems cheap and vulgar to me now."

"Come on, Peg," Eric said, pleading, "let's go out to Benson's like we used to do on Friday nights. They've got a slick orchestra from Denver."

"I can't, Eric," she said.

"But there isn't a rough crowd out there tonight. It's always a bunch of high school kids on Friday nights."

"I know, Eric," she told him, "but I still can't go."

"Why not?" he demanded petulantly.

"We've been all over that," she explained. "You know when I gave my heart to Jesus that I gave up all those things to live for Him. I can't go dancing with you tonight or any other night."

"All right," he pouted, "so you think more of that stuff than you do of me."

"It isn't that, Eric," she said, her voice trembling. "Can't you understand?"

"I've gone to church with you," he persisted. "The least you could do is to go out to Benson's with me. Especially when we'd both have so much fun."

"It doesn't do any good to talk about it, Eric," she said desperately. "I just can't go out there with you."

"All right. All right," he answered, his voice harsh, "if you don't want to go where I do, that's all right. Just have your own way!"

About the same time Larry and Danny walked up onto the porch of Coach Edward's home.

"I thought you fellows would be home and in bed," the coach said pointedly.

"We would have been," Danny answered, "but we've just got to talk to you for a little while tonight."

"Okay." The coach showed them into the living room.

When they were inside and seated, Larry blurted out his story.

"When did you say that happened?" Coach Edwards asked.

"Just a few minutes ago," Danny put in. "We thought we'd better come right over and talk to you about it."

"You did the right thing," the coach replied. "This is serious. More serious than you know." He thought a minute. "Don't say a word about this to anyone, fellows, not even to your folks or your best friends. We've got to do something to put a stop to this before those guys get hold of one of the fellows who might let himself get talked into helping them."

"We won't mention it to anyone," they both promised.

"I hope you will be willing to help us, too," Mr. Edwards went on. "It might be dangerous, but they made their first contacts with you. It may be that you'll be the only ones who will be able to help us trap them."

Danny and Larry looked at one another for a moment, then both nodded solemnly.

"We'll help you," they said.

Chapter 11

IMPOSSIBLE TO LIE

THE NEXT MORNING when Danny and Larry entered the schoolhouse Coach Edwards was standing at the door waiting for them.

"There you are, fellows," he said, falling into step beside them. "I've got some things I'd like to go over with you. Let's go up to the office."

"Okay," they answered.

"You played a good game, Larry," one of the kids called to him as he went up the steps.

Larry grinned happily. It was good to be recognized as one of the fellows again.

The coach walked on ahead, ushered them into his private office, shut the door, and locked it carefully. There in the chair beside the desk sat tall, lanky Sheriff Riley. Danny could feel his heart start to pound, and the color drain from his face. He looked over at his cousin, whose shoulders and hands were trembling.

"How are you, boys?" the sheriff asked pleasantly.

"F-f-fine, thank you," Danny replied.

"I've been hearing some good reports about you, Larry," he went on. "I'm glad to know that you're doing so well."

For a moment or two there was a strained silence. The school bell rang and the corridor was filled at once with the sound of countless voices and hurrying footsteps.

"After you boys left my house last night, I called the sheriff," Coach Edwards said, keeping his voice low, "and talked with him about your visit. He suggested that the four of us get together this morning and go over the whole affair from the beginning."

"Yes," Sheriff Riley put in, "this could be a great deal more serious than it sounds on the surface. It might be just a little two-bit gambler who wants to pick up an extra fifty dollars. If it is, we can take care of that easily enough. But it might be something like what happened in college basketball, where organized crime moved in. That's an entirely different matter." He crossed his legs and took a notebook from his pocket. "That's what we've got to find out."

Slowly and carefully the boys went over the events of the whole evening, telling how Woody Blackburn and a stranger in a big convertible had stopped Larry and sounded him out on throwing the game for them.

"Had you ever seen Woody's companion before?" the sheriff asked.

"No," Larry replied. "I didn't get a very good look at him, either. Only I know he was a lot older than Woody. I think he had a tiny gray mustache."

"It sounds like the work of someone a little older," Coach Edwards put in. "We've got to stop this, sheriff. This thing could ruin football here in Iron Mountain, and perhaps in the whole Conference, if we don't."

"That's right," Mr. Riley answered. "And if it works here, it'll spread to other sports, and perhaps trap a lot of foolish boys who think they'd like to pick up some easy money. It would ruin every boy it touched." He turned to Larry and Danny. "The only thing, fellows, is that we don't have any real evidence, not the kind that would hold up in court. That's the reason why we wanted to talk to you."

"What do you want us to do?" Larry asked.

"We want you to let those fellows contact you, and perhaps let them think that you're going to help them," Coach Edwards explained. "Then you can keep your eyes open and try to get a line on who the real leader is and just what they are planning to do. If they'll give you some money to throw that game, so much the better. Then we'll have them for sure."

The boys were silent for a moment.

"You wouldn't expect us to lie to them, would you, Coach Edwards?" Larry asked momentarily. "You wouldn't expect us to tell them that we'd actually throw a game, would you?"

"What difference would that make?" Coach Edwards asked. "They're only a couple of crooks. Why would it matter what sort of lies you had to tell them?"

"It would make a lot of difference," Larry went on. "It isn't Christian to lie, even to fellows like Woody and his companion."

The sheriff and coach looked at one another queerly.

"If you feel that way about lying, son," Sheriff Riley said, "after the way you were a few months ago, I surely wouldn't want you to lie. You just keep still and let them do the talking. I don't think you'll have to say anything that isn't true."

When the interview was finally over and the coach opened the door to let the boys out into the hallway, Danny turned to his cousin.

"Boy," he said softly as they hurried along the corridor toward their first class, "this is really something, isn't it?"

"Yes," Larry replied. "And I'm scared. That Woody Blackburn is big enough to make two of either of us. And he was the toughest bully in the reformatory. If–if he ever finds out about this, we're both done for."

"But we couldn't do any differently," Danny told him. "We've got to help do what we can to get those fellows before they talk someone else into helping them."

"I know that's right," Larry replied thoughtfully. "But it scares me just to think about it."

All during the week Larry alternated with Eric Tanner at end. The older boy buckled down to work after his second scrimmage on the side lines and began to look more like he had at the first of the season.

"I'm going to move you over to left half, Larry," the coach told him after the Thursday night session. "If Eric comes through, as it looks as though he's going to, we'll put him back at end. I think you'll be more valuable to us in the backfield anyway."

"Fine," Larry said. "I don't care where I play, just so I get to play."

Chapter 12

CHRISTIAN TESTIMONY, A MUST

THE GAMBLERS didn't make an attempt to contact either Larry or Danny all through the week. It was almost as though the whole affair had been a dream, a black, ugly nightmare that had never actually happened at all.

"Maybe they decided that Iron Mountain didn't look like a good place to try their dirty work, after all," Larry said hopefully as he and Danny walked out to the schoolhouse before the game Friday evening. "And it sure wouldn't make me feel bad if they did."

"Me neither," the young woodsman repeated fervently.

Larry and Danny had another big night against Winston. Between them they passed and ran the defensive team silly, and scored three touchdowns before Coach Edwards pulled them out.

"You guys have done enough for the night," he chuckled. "I think we ought to give the reserves a chance to show what they can do."

When the game was finally over, the boys had their showers and dressed, then they went out into the chill October air.

Peggy was sitting in Eric Tanner's old car waiting for him. "Hi, fellows," she said, waving gaily. "Have you seen Eric?"

"I think he left quite a little while ago," Danny replied. "I know he wasn't in the locker room when I came out."

"He asked me to drive his car over here and wait for him," she said. "But he's surely had time enough to take a shower and change clothes."

Larry turned around. "Oh, here he comes now."

Eric scowled at them as he came up to the car, but he didn't speak. Danny and Larry turned off and went up the street.

"What'd those two guys want, Peg?" he demanded angrily as he climbed into the car beside her and started the motor.

"They just stopped to talk to me a minute," she said. "In fact, I called them over and asked them if they had seen you."

"I wish they'd leave you alone," he snapped, slamming the car into gear. "I just don't like it."

"You shouldn't be jealous of them, Eric," she told him.

"Jealous?" he repeated scornfully. "You wouldn't catch me being jealous of a couple of punks like that."

They drove around for awhile, out by the old ball park, past the swimming pool, and down the street where Peggy lived.

"Boy, this is some night, isn't it?" Eric said, looking out at the starlit sky. "This is the best time of the year, isn't it?"

"It would be perfect," she said slowly, "if only——"

"If only what?" he cut in, anger tinging his voice.

"If only you would take Jesus as your Saviour, Eric," she said. "You have no idea how wonderful it really is to be a Christian! Just to know that the sin question is settled in your life, and to put your trust in Him for salvation is a marvelous experience. If you did that, Eric, then everything would be perfect."

"You talk as though I'm a gangster or something," he told her. "I haven't been as wicked as all that. I haven't done so much sinning that I need a Saviour."

"The Bible tells us," she went on seriously, "that everyone has sinned and has come short of the glory of God; that we are all like sheep who have gone astray. That means you and me, Eric, as well as the worst sinners in the world."

"I don't get it," Eric Tanner snapped, his voice

rising. He drove on in silence for several minutes.

Once or twice Peggy started to speak, then stopped and sat quietly, her lips moving in prayer.

"I might take you up on that some time, Peg," he said huskily at last, "but right now, I'm going to have my fun. I want to get out and see a little of the world and enjoy myself. Then, perhaps I'll be ready to become a Christian."

"You might not get the chance, Eric," she told him quietly.

"Oh, now, I'm not so old that I'm going to kick in right yet," he laughed. "I'll tell you what, Peg. You go out to Benson's Dine and Dance with me tonight, and I'll go to church on Sunday with you."

"But I can't do that, Eric," she protested. "I wouldn't feel right going to a place like that now."

"You won't have to dance," he told her. "I just want to see a couple of fellows. They've got a little deal that they want me to help them on."

"What sort of a deal?" she asked.

"Just a deal." His mouth drew down to a thin, narrow line. "A deal where I can make some easy dough. We won't be out there more than half an hour."

"No, Eric," she said softly.

"Then I'll have to take you home," he snorted. "You've certainly become a wet blanket all of a sudden, when you won't even go with me out to Benson's for a few minutes on business."

Peggy didn't say any more until they reached her home. Eric reached across her and opened the door.

"Aren't you even going to walk up to the door with me?" she asked hesitantly.

"I'm in a hurry," he retorted, bristling. "You've made me late already—you and this crazy religion business!"

Peggy stood there watching while he grated the old engine into gear and with a roar went careening down the street. Then she turned and fled into the house. Hot tears were spilling down her cheeks.

In the meantime Danny and Larry walked slowly down the street, talking about the football game they had just played and the one that was coming up the following week end, when the same convertible pulled up beside them. Neither of them noticed it until Woody called out to Larry.

"Hey," he sang out imperiously, "come over here a minute, will you, fella?"

Both Danny and Larry straightened suddenly at the sound of the strident voice and whirled quickly to see the long, low car.

For a moment or two Larry hesitated, the sweat coming out on his forehead.

"It's me, Woody," one of the men called a second time. "Both of you come here, just for a minute. We'd like to talk to you."

"Okay," Larry managed.

Danny's heart was hammering a fierce tattoo in his throat as he and his cousin approached the darkened car.

"Say," Woody said as they came up to where he was sitting, "you guys really played a swell game tonight. As good as anything I've seen in high school."

"You can say that again," the older man put in. "You looked like a pair of pros."

"Everything went pretty good for us," Danny said.

"Don't be so modest," he continued. "The two of you won that game for Iron Mountain by yourselves."

There was an embarrassed silence.

"Some day you might get paid for playing football," Woody said. "Have you ever thought of that?"

"Not very much," Danny answered.

"In fact, you might not have to wait so long," the older boy said, grinning evilly. "Have you thought any more about our proposition?" Woody asked.

"A little," Larry told him.

"What did you decide?"

But his companion cut in quickly. "While you're thinking it over," he said, "why don't you take in a show on us and let us show you a good time?"

"We don't go to shows," Larry replied. "And I–I don't know whether we'd go for your kind of a good time or not."

"What's the matter with shows?" Woody demanded.

"We're Christians," Larry said simply.

Woody Blackburn was silent for a moment. Then he started to laugh. "Say," he exclaimed, "that's the best dodge that I've heard of yet. Nobody would suspect you if you don't even go to shows or smoke. This is perfect."

"Well, we'll be seeing you in a couple of days, fellows," Woody's companion said, starting the motor. "We've got to run along now. We've got to meet a guy on business out at Benson's Dine and Dance."

Chapter 13

A PAST HARD TO LIVE DOWN

"MAN, OH, MAN," Larry exclaimed when they were alone again. "What do you make of that?"

Danny took a deep breath and tried hard to keep his voice from showing the tense excitement that he felt. "It sounds to me as though those guys really think we're going to help them," he said. "And I don't think it's any little deal. They're much too anxious for that."

Larry looked apprehensively up the dark street and to the east in the direction the convertible had gone, as though he half expected them to return.

"I'll tell you, the cold shivers ran up and down my spine all the time we were talking to them," he said. "What–what do you suppose we ought to do now?"

"The only thing we can do is to wait," Danny told him. "We don't actually have any more evidence at all. In fact, we don't know any more than we did before."

"Except that they've contacted someone else," Larry added, "or are planning to."

"We've just got to help catch them," Danny said determinedly. "Sheriff Riley is right. If they talk any of the fellows into throwing the game it could just ruin his whole life!"

The boys had expected Woody and his companion to get in touch with them again within the next night or two, but Saturday and Sunday came and went, and there was no sign of them.

On Sunday morning something happened that made Larry jubilant. One of the junior class Sunday school teachers stopped him in the church basement.

"Say, Larry," the teacher began. "I've been wanting to get hold of you for the past week. What do you do on Saturday mornings?"

"Just a few chores around the house," he replied. "I've been trying to get a job, but with football and all I haven't been able to find anything."

"My class of boys want to get together every Saturday morning to play a little football and basketball," the teacher went on. "I don't have the time to go over and supervise them, but I thought perhaps you would."

"Do you mean that you'd like to have me go over and help with them?" Larry echoed, beaming.

Mr. Carlson nodded. "I surely would."

"I'd really like it," Larry told him.

"Fine," the teacher answered. "I'll tell the gang. I know they're all going to be glad that we've found someone."

Larry could scarcely wait until church was over so he could tell Danny Orlis what had happened.

"Just think," he said as soon as they were out on the church steps. "Mr. Carlson wants me to take charge of his class of boys for some games on Saturday morning. That shows that people are beginning to trust me again."

"That's swell," Danny replied. "He certainly wouldn't ask you to take charge of a group of boys from his class if he wasn't positive that you had changed."

"You don't know how happy that makes me feel," Larry went on. "Maybe if I get out there a little early I'll have a chance to testify to some of the kids before we begin. I can tell them that I know what it's like to serve Satan, and that there isn't any happiness or contentment in it. I can tell them how a fellow has to pay for sin and——"

Danny grasped Larry's arm and squeezed it hard. "Did you see who just went by in that convertible?" he broke in.

"Woody?" Larry asked tensely.

"Woody and two other fellows," Danny said. "One of them was that same guy who's been with him when he talked to us, but I didn't get a good look at the other fellow."

"You–you don't suppose they're looking for us, do you?" he asked.

Danny shook his head. "He waved and smiled, but that was all. He didn't even act as though he was going to stop."

Larry sighed deeply. "I'm just as glad he didn't," he said.

On Monday after school Coach Edwards ran the squad through a light scrimmage, then called them over to one corner of the field and had them sit down.

"Well, fellows," he said, "we've got a big game coming up this week. We're going to meet good, solid tackling and a lightning offense for the first time this season. I'm going to have to demand the best from each one of you." He stopped and looked from one to the other. "I hope that every man on our squad is honorable," he went on. "I hope that we don't have a single fellow who would give less than his best to the team, regardless of what pressure was brought to bear upon him."

Danny thought for a moment that Coach Edwards was going to tell the whole story of how the two gamblers approached Larry and him. The boys looked at one another, not understanding what their coach meant. But Coach Edwards went on to the mistakes of the Friday night game without offering any further explanation. When he finally finished and dismissed them for the night, he called Larry and Danny to one side.

"Any news?" he asked softly.

Danny shook his head.

"They stopped us on the way home from the game Friday night and talked with us for a few minutes," Larry told him, "but they didn't say much of anything different, except that they wanted to help us get some easy money."

"If you get any real dope let the sheriff or me know right away," the coach went on. "We're working on the case from every angle, but so far we haven't got too much to go on. It's really got me worried, fellows. I'm afraid they might get next to one of the guys who would listen to them."

"We'll surely get in touch with you," Danny said.

"And whatever you do," the coach warned, "be careful."

When they got home from school that evening Bob said, "Say, Larry, you're supposed to call Mrs. Kimball right away."

"Who's Mrs. Kimball?" he asked.

"Search me," his brother replied, "but she sounded as though it was mighty important. She told me two or three times that she wanted me to be sure and see that you phoned her this evening as soon as you got home."

Larry went to the phone and called the number that Bob had written on the pad. He talked for several minutes. When he finished, he set the phone down and, white faced and trembling, he brushed past Bob and started for the basement where Danny was studying.

"What did she want?" Bob asked curiously.

"Oh, her boy is in the junior class at Sunday school. That's the class I'm going to look out for on Saturdays when they play football and basketball," he explained.

"She sounded awfully excited for something like that," Bob observed.

Larry went on down to the basement and into Danny's room without saying anything more to his brother.

"I–I thought perhaps everyone had forgotten about my–my trouble," he said. Danny could see that his cousin's lip was quivering uncertainly.

"What do you mean?" he asked.

"I just had a telephone call from a Mrs. Kimball," Larry said. "Her boy is in that class I'm supposed to supervise. She just heard that I was going to be in charge of the games on Saturday, and she called and wanted to find out about it. She–she said that she didn't feel that a boy who had been in the reform school had any business working with a group of younger fellows!"

Chapter 14

BETTING ON THE WINNER

FOR A MOMENT OR TWO Danny and Larry stood there, staring at one another silently. Larry moved over to the dresser and fingered the Bible that was lying upon it. The color had drained from his cheeks and his fingers were trembling.

"What did you tell Mrs. Kimball?" Danny asked at last.

"I told her that I had been saved," Larry went on, "and that Christ had changed my life, that I didn't do any of the things I had been doing before. She seemed to feel a little better about it."

"That's good," the young woodsman replied.

"Oh, Danny," he exclaimed, "if I could just make these kids see where they're headed when they serve Satan. If they could just see the suffering and shame and heartache that's ahead for them if they don't take the Lord Jesus Christ as their Saviour!"

"I'll be praying for you as you try to deal with them, fellow," Danny said, smiling. It was so good to see his cousin concerned about the souls of others instead of thinking of himself continuously.

That night after supper the two boys were just getting ready to go to the library when the telephone rang once more. This time it was Woody.

"Are you and your pal going to be out for a little while tonight, Larry?" he asked.

"We're going down to the library to do some outside reading for history," Larry told him.

"Swell," Woody replied. "We're in a drugstore about six blocks from where you live. Start out for the library and we'll pick you up. Okay?"

Larry looked first one way and then the other to be sure no one was listening. Then he whispered, "It's them, Danny. They want to take us to the library."

They went out of the house together and had only walked about half a block when the big convertible again pulled up beside them.

"Hop in," Woody said pleasantly. "We'll give you a lift."

"I—I don't think we'd better," Danny protested. "Somebody might see us."

"Maybe you're right at that," the older man answered. "This is a secluded spot. No one will see us with you if we stay here."

"Our plans are all made," Woody put in quickly. "We're going to clean up, and so are you."

"Just what is it that you want us to do?" Danny asked hesitantly.

"How badly do you want to win that game with Spring Creek?" Woody asked, grinning.

"It means an awful lot," Larry said truthfully.

"A hundred dollars' worth?" the older man put in. "A hundred apiece, I mean."

The boys stood there looking at one another uncertainly.

"You won't need to worry any," Woody said. "All you'll have to do is to drop a couple of passes, or miss a tackle when it'll do the most good. Nobody will be the wiser."

"We're lining up another guy, too," the other man said, "so you won't have to do it all. You won't have to worry about looking too bad."

The gamblers took Larry and Danny's silence for acceptance.

"You know, Larry," Woody continued, "this game has been getting a big play in the papers all over the state. Both teams are rated as the two best in Colorado. There is going to be a lot of betting on it." He winked broadly. "And we're going to be betting on the winner."

His companion leaned forward and looked up the street at a pair of headlights approaching them.

"Well, Woody," he said, "if everything is set, we'd better be on our way. We've got that other guy to meet out at Benson's. We don't want to be late and miss him, and we don't want to be seen here talking to Larry and his friend."

"He won't be there until half-past nine," Woody said. "And besides, he'll wait for us."

"Just the same, I think we'd better be on our way. So long, fellows," he said. Then he lowered his voice and leaned toward them. "You know I'm an easy fellow to get along with," he whispered, "but nobody backs out on a deal with me." With that he meshed the gears quietly and the car moved away.

When they were gone, Danny turned to Larry.

"Now we are in for it," he explained. "Let's go back to the house and phone Coach Edwards quick."

But Larry hesitated. "I don't think we'd better right now," he said. "Woody doesn't trust anyone. They might take a swing back around here to see where we go and what we do."

Sure enough. As they turned in at the library Danny caught a glimpse of the convertible creeping by.

Coach Edwards wasn't at home when the boys finally got to a place where they could phone him, and neither was Sheriff Riley.

"What'll we do now?" Larry asked.

"Listen," Danny said. "We've got to find out

who this other fellow on the team is that they've made a deal with, and tonight might be the only chance that we'll get."

"You—you don't mean that we ought to go out to Benson's, do you?" Larry asked hesitantly. "That's a tough place."

"That's the only way that we can possibly be sure," he said.

"But Danny," Larry countered, "if those fellows catch us, it'll just be too bad for us!"

"We'll have to see that they don't catch us, then," the young woodsman said softly.

Chapter 15

JUDGE NOT BY APPEARANCES

I DON'T KNOW," Larry said uncertainly, "whether we ought to go out to Benson's tonight or not."

"But we've got to go," Danny told him. "We don't have any choice. We can't find the sheriff or Coach Edwards, and somebody has got to get out there and find out the name of the football player they're contacting there tonight."

Larry took a deep breath. "I guess we did promise that we'd do what we could to help catch these fellows," he said reluctantly.

"And it's only a mile or so out there," Danny continued. "We can walk it and get back to town long before ten o'clock. We don't have to worry about that."

"I know," Larry answered. "That isn't what I am worried about. It's Woody and his pal. If they come along while we're walking on the road, we'll really be in trouble. They'll know right away where we're going, and perhaps they'll guess why."

"It's dark," Danny replied, "and the road is so

crooked that they'll have to drive with their headlights on, even if they didn't want to. We can duck into the brush at the side of the road every time we see somebody coming."

Larry gulped hard.

"I—I suppose we've got to," he said, "but I can tell you this much, I certainly wouldn't want that pal of Woody's to find out what we're doing. He—he looked to me like the kind of a guy who'd take a good healthy poke at a fellow as quick as he'd look at him."

"You think of the nicest things." Danny laughed.

They walked down the long, shady street to the narrow graveled road that led up to Benson's Dine and Dance, a dirty little roadhouse which was built outside of town so that it wouldn't be subject to the regulations the city placed on such taverns.

"We'll stay on the road until we get close enough to see the place," Danny said. "Then we'll sneak off into the brush and come up on the hill behind it."

"If we'd go over on the south side we could get up high enough to look right into the windows and see most of the booths and the dance floor," Larry said. "I used to do it all the time."

"That sounds like a good idea," Danny told him.

As they walked under the last street light a gray sedan crept slowly past them.

"Did you see that car?" Larry asked, starting a little.

"Certainly I saw it," the young woodsman replied, "but it wasn't a convertible. That wasn't Woody and his friend."

"Just the same," his cousin continued, "that car has passed us twice at least, going real slow, just as it did that time. I think they're spying on us."

"Boy, now you are imagining things," Danny scoffed.

It was dark out on the narrow road to the Dine and Dance. The trees closed in on either side and almost met overhead to form a roof of green.

"I never did notice before that it was this dark out here," Larry said, looking from one side to the other.

Danny laughed easily. He was used to finding his way around in the pitch blackness of the Lake of the Woods when clouds blotted out the moon and stars, and all was darkness and emptiness about him.

"It's getting sort of late," the young woodsman said. "I certainly hope that we——"

He didn't get to finish the sentence. At that very instant they were bathed in light, silhouetted in sharp relief against the curtain of darkness.

"Danny!" Larry cried, terror in his voice. "What'll we do?"

For a split second they stood there, like deer frozen in the blazing spotlight of a "shiner." Then they whirled and dashed for the brush.

"You needn't run, Larry Anders!" a sharp, crisp voice rang out. "We've seen you. We know where you're going." There was the grating noise of hastily meshed gears. "And you call yourself a Christian!"

"Mrs. Kimball!" Larry exclaimed in dismay. "Now I am in for it!"

Danny stood there, staring after the rapidly vanishing tail light. His heart was still hammering against his ribs and a thin line of sweat beaded his forehead.

"Whew!" he exclaimed weakly.

"I thought sure Woody and his buddy had us," Larry managed. "I could just feel that guy's big first on my shoulder."

"Mrs. Kimball must have seen us in town," Danny said. "And followed us out here with her lights out so that she could be sure to catch us."

"And I know why," Larry answered. He thought suddenly of the class of junior boys he wanted to work with. "She—she'll never believe me now."

While they were standing there talking headlights appeared around a bend two or three hundred yards ahead and raced toward them.

"Quick, Larry!" Danny shouted. "Into the brush!"

They both dove for the ditch. And not an instant too soon. They had scarcely flattened against the sand and rocks when powerful headlights bathed the road in light, and swept on to leave them in darkness once more.

"That was close," Larry breathed when he could talk again.

"You aren't kidding," Danny replied. "That was Woody's convertible."

"Do—do you think they saw us?" his cousin asked excitedly.

Danny shook his head. "They were in too big a hurry to see anything but the road," he answered. "And besides, we were down in the brush when they went by."

Larry shivered involuntarily. "And now," he said in disgust, "we won't even be able to see whom they came out here to meet."

"Nobody else has gone," Danny replied. "If we hurry, we can see if there's a member of the team out here. That wouldn't be evidence at all, but it would give us an idea of whom to watch."

They reached the notorious Dine and Dance and sneaked through the trees around to the hill on the south side of the low, rambling building.

Chapter 16

NO POSITIVE CLUE YET

BE CAREFUL NOW," Danny whispered. "We still don't want to be caught out here, even if Woody and his friend are gone."

"You aren't telling me anything," Larry answered in a hushed monotone.

There were quite a number of people in the dimly lighted building and Danny and Larry crept closer to the windows.

"Do you see anybody?" his cousin asked tensely.

A moment or so later Danny grasped his arm. "There's Toby Walters and Fred Brady and Mickey Jones," he said, "they're all sitting in that booth in the corner."

"And over at the counter is Spike Morgan," Larry added. "It–it couldn't be all four of them, could it?" he asked.

"I just don't know what to think," Danny answered. "Come on, let's get out of here."

They walked in silence most of the way home. Finally Danny said, "It might be that Woody got out there and saw so many of the team that they didn't even try to contact their man tonight. You know how careful they were about being seen talking to us."

"They did leave awfully early," Larry agreed, "for having spent time talking to anybody."

The next morning at school the boys reported to Coach Edwards what had happened the night before.

"We tried to call both you and the sheriff," Danny explained, "but we couldn't get either one of you."

"We weren't at home," Coach Edwards said. "We got a phony tip yesterday afternoon and made a wild goose chase to Denver before we learned that there was nothing to it." He ran his fingers nervously through his hair. "I've been so afraid that those two would get their dirty hands on some of the other fellows that I haven't known what to do. That's one reason why the sheriff and I have been so anxious to get to the bottom of it."

Danny and Larry hadn't told him about the four fellows they had seen out at Benson's. They didn't have any real evidence that any of them were involved and Larry had been determined to have some real evidence that would hold up in court before he turned their names in to Coach Edwards or the sheriff.

"Keep your eyes and ears open," the coach said to them once more as they went back out into the hall. "Perhaps the sheriff and I will be around the next time we get a little break."

At noon when Larry got home from school Mr. Bigelow, the Junior Department Sunday school teacher, was there waiting to talk with him.

"I had a telephone call you may be able to explain, Larry," he said softly. "Mrs. Kimball called and said that she had seen you and Danny walking out to Benson's Dine and Dance last night."

"I—I—" Larry swallowed hard. "I guess that's true," he said hesitantly, "but we weren't going inside."

"Would you mind telling me just why you did go out there?" the teacher continued. "I'd like to have something to tell Mrs. Kimball."

"I—I can't, Mr. Bigelow," he said. "I might be able to explain to you a little later, but I–I just can't right now."

Mr. Bigelow fingered his hat thoughtfully.

"I was hoping that I'd get a more satisfactory answer, Larry," he said. "I told Mrs. Kimball that I was certain I could phone her this afternoon and explain the situation adequately to her." He paused for a moment or two. "You know, of course," he went on slowly, "that we're not going to be able to let you take charge of the boys' Saturday program until we do get a satisfactory explanation of your going out there. We just can't have a person in charge of our boys who frequents a place like Benson's."

"I know that, Mr. Bigelow," Larry answered.

When he was gone, Danny came into the living room.

"Boy, that's tough," he said. "And the worst of it is that we can't explain to them, either."

Larry was silent for a long while. Finally, he looked up and said, "When a guy gets a bad reputation, it surely takes a long time to live it down, doesn't it? If I hadn't been in the reformatory once, Mrs. Kimball probably would never have followed us. And anyway, Mr. Bigelow would have taken my word that we weren't going out there to go inside like so many of the kids do."

"I think you're right about that," Danny told him. "But the thing you must do now is to live so carefully that they won't have anything to talk about."

That night at Young Peoples, Peggy came over and talked with Danny again.

"I—I hate to be coming to you like this all the time," she said, "but I've got to have somebody to talk with."

She stopped for a moment, and Danny thought she was going to cry.

"Danny," she went on when she could speak, "I'm miserable."

"Is it because of Eric?" he asked.

"How did you know?" she retorted quickly.

"I don't know," he told her. "I just sort of figured that it was. He isn't a Christian, and you are. That's enough to cause all kinds of trouble."

"I wish I'd quit going with him right after I had accepted Christ," she said brokenly. "It–it would have been so much easier then."

"Perhaps that would still be the best," Danny suggested.

"But Danny," she replied, "I–I like him so much."

The young woodsman took his Testament from his pocket and fingered it, trying to remember a verse that would help her.

"I thought that I could win him for Christ," she went on, "but he's farther away now than ever. Last night when he came over he was terribly late and he–he'd been drinking, I think. He smelled like it, anyway. And all he could do was boast about the big time he had had, and all the easy money he was going to make."

"Easy money?" Danny echoed. "What did he mean by that?"

"He didn't say," she went on, "but he was awfully excited about it."

Chapter 17

PRACTICE AND DECISIONS COME HARDER

As soon as the meeting was over and Danny and Larry were alone together, the young woodsman told Larry what Peggy had said.

He whistled in amazement. "Do you suppose that Eric really is the guy?" he asked.

"It certainly looks suspicious," Danny replied. "He's one of the best players on the team and he'd be in position to throw a game if he'd want to."

"But I can't figure out why we didn't see him out at Benson's then?" Larry continued. "If he's the guy, he should have been out there."

"I've been wondering about that myself." Danny stopped a moment and began to pull thoughtfully at the lobe of his ear. "It could be," he said, "that Eric was in the car with Woody. You know they wanted to take us out and show us what they called a good time. Perhaps he took them up on it."

"That makes sense," his cousin said. "And he left with them before we got there."

"What will we do, Larry?" the young woodsman

asked. "Should we go and see the sheriff and Coach Edwards and tell them what we suspect?"

Larry Anders shook his head. "Let's get some real proof before we say anything to anyone," he answered. "I've been through that. It's bad enough when a fellow's guilty."

"I think you've got something there," Danny told him.

"If we could just think of something that would help us get the evidence that we need," Larry said.

Although the football team had won every game they had played thus far, things weren't going too well with the squad. Danny could tell as much by the indifferent way the fellows blocked and the sloppy execution of plays during scrimmage. Every now and then an alert reserve lineman would filter through and smack the ball carrier for a ten- or twelve-yard loss. Coach Edwards noticed it, too. He stopped the scrimmage and called the squad together.

"What's the matter with you fellows?" he demanded. "Some of you tackle like you're playing 'drop the handkerchief.' " He stopped and looked the fellows over critically. "Mickey—Spike—Tubby," he said. "Where were you guys last night?"

"H–home, I think," one of them answered, glancing nervously at the others. "Why?"

"You don't play as though you'd been home in bed when you should have," the coach went on. "You act as though you'd been out half the night."

"Oh, we were in early," the spokesman countered. "Weren't we, fellows?"

The others nodded in agreement.

"I'm not going to ask you what time you got in," Coach Edwards replied, "but I am going to tell you this much: if I catch one of you—I don't care who he is—out after ten o'clock, he goes off the squad. We've got a good team this year, but we don't have the championship yet. And if you fellows don't buckle down and get to work, we're not going to win."

When the practice was finally over, Eric dressed and walked down to the drugstore with Peggy for a soda.

"That lame-brained coach!" he retorted angrily. "If he thinks I'm going to be in at any ten o'clock every night, he's got another guess coming."

"But Eric," Peggy countered, "we want to win that game. We've just got to."

He looked at her queerly. "It's just another football game."

"Eric!" she exclaimed. "What's come over you? You never used to talk like that."

"Nothing's come over me," he snapped. "You're the one who's so queer. If you aren't hounding me about your old religion, you're after me about doing as 'coachie says,' and getting to bed early. I'm about fed up."

Tears came to Peggy's eyes, but she did not answer.

Eric finished his soda and picked up the check. "There's a peach of a show on tonight, Peg," he said, softening suddenly. "How about taking it in with me?"

"Eric," she said hesitantly, "don't ask me to. It just causes trouble."

"We used to have so much fun," he went on. "Now you're so sanctimonious that you won't do anything with me any more."

Peggy took a deep breath. "Oh, Eric," she said, "it isn't any use. We—we can't make a go of it any more."

Eric had started toward the cashier's desk. Now he came back and sat down.

"Don't start that again, Peg," he said irritably.

"But it's true, Eric," she went on. "Our ideals are different. Our ideas of good times are different, and we can't be together for ten minutes any more without fighting about something."

"Sure, we can get along," Eric replied easily. "All you've got to do is to drop some of your old-fogey ideas and just be a little more like you used to be. Then we'll get along fine."

"But don't you understand, Eric?" she pleaded. "I can't do that. I'm a Christian now."

"Don't start to cry, Peggy," he said quickly. "We'll make a deal. I won't ask you to go with me to the theater or dances or places like that, and you quit asking me to become a Christian. We'll compromise. How about it?"

"It wouldn't work," she said softly. "I—I don't think that we'd better go together, for awhile, anyway."

Eric straightened and his eyes flashed. "Listen, Peggy," he said, "if you quit going with me for a little while, we're through for good. If I'm not good enough to go with you for a month, I'm not good enough to go with you at all."

"I—I don't know what to do, Eric," she said miserably, "I'm all mixed up."

On the Tuesday evening before the big game, a little boy came up to Larry's home and handed him a note.

"A big tall guy gave me a quarter to bring you this," he said importantly.

Larry took the note and opened it.

"What do you make of it, Danny?" he asked at last, his hand trembling as he thrust the note at his cousin.

"Must see you tomorrow," the note said. "Phone

me at number 301 as to time and place." Signed, "Woody."

Danny felt the sweat come out on his forehead.

Chapter 18

THE PLAN WORKS

"THIS IS IT," the young woodsman said slowly, reading the note again. "They—they want to give us our final instructions for throwing the game."

Larry took the note and read it again, as though he still couldn't believe what it had said.

"But what are we going to do?" he asked plaintively. "What are we going to do?'

"We'd better get hold of Coach Edwards or the sheriff right away," Danny told him. "We've got to have help on this."

His cousin was silent for two or three minutes. "If there was just some way that we could get the evidence on them," he said slowly, "the sort of evidence that would put them in jail where they belong." He stared off into space, almost blankly. "I've got it!" he cried. "Do you think we could lure them over here to the house?"

"I don't know," Danny replied. "Why would you want them over here?"

"The folks are going to be gone tomorrow night," Larry said. "If we could get them over here, down the basement in your room, we could plant my tape recorder under the bed, or behind the big chair and get everything down. Then we'd have them."

"Say," Danny exclaimed. "That's a swell idea."

"That would give us some evidence that would tear down any defense they might have," he continued. "With that to play back to them Sheriff Riley could get his confession easily enough."

The boys hurried down into Danny's basement room and set up the tape recorder with an hour spool of tape.

"We've got to get it hidden now," Danny said. "How about over there in a dresser drawer?"

"Fine," Danny replied. "Then we can run the mike wire out through the back and over here behind these two chairs."

"Oh, boy!" Danny chuckled. "Won't Woody and his pal get a surprise when they hear this tape played back to them in jail?"

"I–I just hope that everything goes the way we've go it planned," Larry said cautiously. "We're going to be here alone with those two fellows."

Larry called 301 early the next morning and talked with Woody. He had a little trouble convincing him that they ought to meet at his house.

"I think we'd better pick you up over by the library about eight o'clock," Woody said.

"It would be a lot safer here at the house."

"And have somebody come busting in and find us there," Woody retorted, "not much."

"But there won't be anybody at home excepting us," Larry persisted. "And besides, I've already told Mother and Dad that I'd be here tonight. If they call and I'm not here to answer the phone, it will be too bad for me."

"Well," Woody said reluctantly. "If that's the way it's got to be, I guess it'll be all right. But I don't mind telling you that I don't like it."

When he hung up Larry said slowly, "Woody acted awfully suspicious all of a sudden."

Uncle Claude and Aunt Lydia Anders left home about seven o'clock, and shortly afterward Bob dressed and went off some place, leaving Larry and Danny alone.

"Is everything okay, Larry?" Danny asked for the fourth or fifth time. "Do you think we ought to check that tape recorder again?"

"We tested it a little while ago," Larry told him. "I know that it's all right."

Danny walked over to the window and looked out. "I just hope that everything goes right tonight," he said nervously.

"Me, too." Larry picked up a magazine and

leafed through it absent-mindedly, then laid it down again. "Danny," he said suddenly, "there's one thing we've forgotten. We haven't prayed about this!"

Together they knelt on the living-room floor. "Dear heavenly Father," the young woodsman began, "You know about all of this. Please be with us and watch over us and care for us. And help us to get the evidence on these two men before they get any of the other fellows started off on the wrong path. And keep us safe, In Jesus' name, Amen."

When Larry had finished praying and they got to their feet, he said, "You know, I think we ought to call the coach and tell him what we're doing."

He picked up the telephone and gave the Edwards' number, but the coach wasn't at home.

"I think he went over to Sheriff Riley's, Larry," Mrs. Edwards said. "You can call him over there."

"Thanks," Larry told her. "I'll do that. It–it's important."

As he set the phone back on the cradle, Danny said excitedly, "Here's Woody and his friend now! You go to the door and I'll dash down and turn on the recorder."

Woody and his tall, scar-faced friend drove up the driveway and into the garage. A moment later they knocked at the back door. Larry showed them down to Danny's room.

"Now listen," Woody's pal said, suspiciously, "I don't like this idea of coming into a house this way. We're going to get right down to business and get out of here as soon as we can."

"Do you boys know what we want you to do?" Woody asked.

"We've got a rough idea," Danny told him, "but you never did go into detail."

"There isn't much detail to it," the older man said. "We're paying you and this other kid to see that Iron Mountain gets beat. We don't care how you do it, just so you make it look good."

"Here's half of your money," Woody said. "When you deliver the goods, you'll get the other half—and a bonus, maybe." He stopped short. "What was that?" he demanded.

"I don't know," his companion retorted irritably. "I don't hear anything. Come on, let's get on with it and get out of here!"

"That squeak!" Woody cried. "It sounds like the squeak of a recording machine. It is! We've been tricked!"

Chapter 19

A DISCOVERY AND RECOVERY

"WE'VE BEEN TRICKED!" Woody cried again.

The older man leaped to his feet. "What do you mean, tricked?" he demanded. His voice was thick with fright and his gaze began to dart frantically from one corner of the room to the other.

"These blasted kids have been playing us for suckers!" Woody retorted. "They've recorded everything we've said."

With a curse the older man snatched the blankets off the bed and kicked the big chair over on its back.

"If it's in here," he cried, "I'll find it." He jerked the mattress off the springs and yanked the dresser out from the wall to peer behind it. "I—I don't see anything, Woody," he shouted excitedly a moment later. "Are you sure?"

"Of course, I'm sure!" the young gambler retorted. He was searching for the tape recorder, too.

"Larry, here, was sent up for illegal radio broadcasting. He's a nut on this sort of stuff."

"We might have known there was something fishy when they insisted that we come down here to talk to them," the other said angrily. "If I find a recorder, I'll tear those blasted kids apart!"

In the excitement Danny touched Larry on the arm and started to sidle toward the door. At the same instant they both started to run for the stairs.

"Grab 'em!" Woody cried. "Grab 'em! If they get away we'll really be in for it!"

Danny was out of the bedroom door first and halfway up the stairs when Larry tripped on the bottom step and went sprawling. With a curse Woody leaped over Larry and grabbed the young woodsman by the leg, jerking him savagely down the steps.

"Now you guys get in here and stay in here!" he ordered, jerking them to their feet and shoving them both along ahead of him. "We're not through with you two. If you try that again, I'll forget to go easy on you!"

Danny rubbed his arms and legs where he had been bruised, bumping down the steps. His heart was hammering fiercely in his throat and his shoulders were quivering. Larry's face was a pasty white and his forehead was beaded with sweat.

"Here's the mike!" Woody's pal exclaimed.

"Now to find that machine!" An instant later he shouted triumphantly as he jerked open the dresser drawer and ripped the tape off the recorder.

"I've got the tape, Woody!" he shouted. "Now let's get out of here!"

For the first time Woody faltered uncertainly. "What about these kids?" he asked. "What are we going to do with them?"

"Take 'em along!" the older man ordered. "I've got a score to settle with them! This whole deal has blown up in our faces and they're going to have to pay for it!"

Woody Blackburn grabbed Larry and Danny by the arms and started shoving them roughly ahead of him. "Get up those steps!" he said menacingly. "And be quick about it!"

"And no funny stuff, either!" his companion ordered.

Once out in the garage the older man shoved past Danny and got in under the wheel of the convertible.

"Hurry up, Woody!" he snapped.

Woody opened the door and flung Danny in beside his companion. "You, Larry, you're going to have to sit on my lap!"

Woody crowded into the seat, jerked Larry down onto his lap and slammed the door. "Now get to going, Jack!" he said tensely. "Let's get out of here, fast!"

"You can say that again!" Jack muttered under his breath.

The motor started with a roar and the gears howled as Jack slammed the car into reverse and started to back up.

At that very moment another car, traveling at a high rate of speed, whirled off the street and into the driveway behind them.

"Look out!" Woody Blackburn shouted.

Jack spiked the brakes, and the car stopped with a lurch that threw Larry into the windshield.

"What the——?" Jack began, starting to crawl out on his side of the convertible.

But Sheriff Riley and Coach Edwards were already at either side of the car.

"What's the trouble?" the sheriff demanded harshly. "What's going on here?"

"These are the men we're looking for!" Coach Edwards exclaimed when he saw Larry and Danny.

At that, Jack started to run, but the sheriff grabbed him roughly by the arm. "Not so fast," he said. "Not so fast. We've got a lot of questions we want to ask you."

"Don't hurt me," Jack whimpered. "Don't hurt me."

"Just behave yourself," Sheriff Riley told him,

"and you won't get hurt." He ran his hands over Jack's pockets. "Hm," he said. "What's this?"

"That's our tape recording," Larry said excitedly. "We had my recorder planted down in Danny's room and took down everything they said to us."

"Well, now," Sheriff Riley smiled, "that's going to make our job of getting a conviction considerably easier."

They all got into the sheriff's car and headed toward the courthouse.

"Boy, it's a good thing you came along when you did!" Danny said. "I don't mind telling you that I was scared. We didn't know what they were going to do to us."

"I guess we can thank my wife for getting us over here," Coach Edwards replied. "After you called for me, she got to worrying and phoned me."

"That just goes to show," Larry said, "how the Lord works things out."

"What do you mean by that, now?" the sheriff asked him.

"Well," Danny replied, "we had decided to handle this thing alone. And when we got our tape recording we were going to bring it over and play it for you. Then, after everything was all set up we prayed that God would guide us and help us. Right afterward, for some reason—we didn't plan it that way at all—I picked the phone up and called you."

"So you see," Larry concluded, "it shows how God answers prayer."

"Well," Coach Edwards answered, "whatever it is, we're glad to have the handcuffs on these two fellows. And we've got you and Larry to thank for it."

Chapter 20

A TRY FOR ESCAPE

IN ANOTHER SECTION OF TOWN Peggy Denton and Eric Tanner were riding slowly down a side street in his car.

"I don't see why going to church and getting a little religion has to make you like you are," Eric said irritably. "A lot of people have religion without going overboard for it like you do."

"But Eric," she told him, "being a Christian isn't being religious, or being anything else, unless you'd say it was being a new person. When you take Christ as your Saviour, you change—you change your attitudes, your sense of right and wrong, your whole way of life."

"Couldn't you use a little common sense about it, though?" he asked. "Take that dance out at Benson's tonight. It wouldn't hurt you to go out there with me for a little while. You don't have to go 'whole hog' on this matter of being a Christian, do you?"

Peggy was silent for a moment or two. Then she

said softly, "You couldn't be just a little bit born, could you? When you were a baby, I mean."

"Of course not," he laughed scornfully. "You'd either be here or you wouldn't. But what's that got to do with it?"

"Well," she went on, "the Bible tells us that becoming a Christian is being born again, only this time into the kingdom of God. It's just like being born on earth. You're either a Christian, or you're not. There isn't any halfway point."

Eric was sitting there biting his lips. "Of all the girls in school who could have goofed off on religion," he said at last, his voice surly, "why did it have to be you?"

Peggy started to speak, then stopped and looked down at her purse. Finally she raised her eyes.

"Eric," she said, striving hard to keep her voice from trembling, "this isn't doing any good. Won't you please take me home?"

"There you go again!" he snapped. With that he leaned forward, switched on the radio and tuned to the local station. "If you feel like that, I will take you home."

"Don't be mad at me," she said brokenly.

A fast, high-pitched recording was on the radio, and Eric turned up the volume.

"At last I can find something that agrees with me," he retorted angrily.

Just then the crisp, cool voice of the announcer broke in. "We interrupt this program of recorded music to bring you a special bulletin from our news room."

Eric swore under his breath, but before he could change the station the announcer went on.

"Sheriff Ben F. Riley and Coach Edwards of our local high school announced a few moments ago that a plot by gamblers to fix the Iron Mountain game for the state football championship has just been uncovered with the active assistance of Larry Anders and Danny Orlis, two members of the team. Two men are being held in the county jail for investigation. Sheriff Riley also announced that his deputies are combing the city for an unidentified member of the football squad who, it is alleged, has accepted a bribe to throw the game."

"Did you hear that?" Peggy asked in surprise. "Who do you suppose it is?"

Eric reached down and switched off the radio. His eyes had taken a furtive, frightened look and the color had drained from his face, leaving it a pale, sickly yellow. Peggy saw that his hands were trembling on the wheel.

"Eric!" she exclaimed. "What's the matter? What's wrong?"

"I've got to get out of here," he said woodenly. "I've go to get out of here!"

And then she understood—understood about his sudden loss of interest in whether they won the game or not; understood where he had gotten the money he had been flashing, and what he meant when he talked about the little deal that was coming off that was going to make him a fistful of easy money.

"Eric!" she cried. "You!"

"I haven't done anything!" He slammed the foot feed of the car to the floor. He whirled around the corner on two wheels, the motor in his old car roaring.

"Eric!" she demanded, suddenly panic-stricken. "Eric! You've got to let me out! You've got to——"

But Peggy didn't have time to finish. She saw the truck lights bearing down upon them, and in an instant saw what was going to happen. She screamed!

Chapter 21

A COSTLY PRICE TO PAY

"LOOK, OUT, ERIC!" Peggy screamed. "Look out!"

Eric Tanner was frozen motionless, his arms stiff and his eyes wide and staring.

Peggy screamed again and threw herself back against the seat, clawing for the door handle. Eric heaved desperately on the wheel, but it was too late! The big truck bore down upon them, brakes screeching! The car lurched wildly as Eric struggled to turn! Suddenly there was a terrifying explosion! That was all Peggy remembered.

The truck driver leaped out of his cab and ran over to the car. "Are you hurt?" he demanded, jerking at the door handle. "Are you hurt?"

For an instant Eric sat there trembling, his hands still on the broken steering wheel.

"Are you hurt?" the truck driver shouted again.

"I–I don't know," Eric stammered.

The truck driver had wrenched the door open by this time, and Eric got out slowly, shaking his head and wiping nervously at his forehead.

"Oh," he moaned, "I guess I don't feel too well." Then he sat down by the side of the road.

Eric didn't seem to remember Peggy until the truck driver played his flashlight on the wreckage and asked, "Were you alone?"

"Peggy!" Eric managed suddenly. "I—I—"

There she lay, crumpled in the corner of the seat with the dashboard jammed and twisted against her legs.

"Here!" the trucker ordered, "we've got to get this girl out of there!" But as he looked, he saw that Eric was stretched out on the ground.

By this time several cars had stopped, and people were crowding about. A doctor pushed his way to the wrecked car just as the driver succeeded in freeing Peggy. He examined them both hurriedly and turned to one of the men.

"Call an ambulance," he said softly. "We've got to get these youngsters to the hospital fast."

"Is Peggy hurt?" Eric mumbled weakly.

The doctor nodded.

"I'm afraid so," he said. "And so are you, young fellow. So just lie here quietly. Don't try to talk. An ambulance will be here soon."

Just then the state troopers drove up and got out of their car, their flashlights in their hands. One of the troopers walked over and put his light on Eric, then Peggy. "These kids look like they've been badly hurt," he said. "The girl is out cold."

"Yes," the doctor said, pointing to Eric, "and I think this young fellow is much worse off than he appears to be. We had better get them to a hospital right away."

Eric moved a little and tried to talk, but the doctor bent over him and said. "Take it easy, lad, you'll need all your strength."

One of the troopers was checking the car for identification. Suddenly he whistled in amazement. "Say, Bill!" he exclaimed to his companion, "this is the kid we got a pick-up order on a little while ago; the football player who was mixed up with those gamblers."

"Well, if he pulls through he'll have plenty to face."

The doctor walked up to the trooper again. "You had better not try to question him," he said, "until we know the extent of his injuries."

The story of the accident spread across town like a forest fire in the hills, but Danny and Larry didn't hear about it until the next morning on the way to school.

"It must have been a terrible accident," the Olson boy who lived across the street from the hospital said breathlessly when he caught up with them. "Peggy's got a broken arm and she must be hurt inside some way. The doctors had to give her a blood transfusion and everything. As first they thought Eric wasn't too badly hurt, but now they don't even know if he's going to live. Dad talked with Dr. Mattson this morning."

"Say, that's too bad," Danny said. He was thinking of the times Peggy had said she couldn't bear to give up Eric, even though he wasn't a Christian. "Perhaps she wouldn't be where she is now," he said to himself, "if she had done as she knew she ought to."

"That certainly is tough. Eric isn't a Christian. If he d-died——" Larry's voice trailed away helplessly.

"Perhaps we can get up to the hospital to see him," Danny put in. "We–we've just got to win him to the Lord——" But the young woodsman couldn't finish. Eric had ever let them talk to him about Christ before. Would he listen now?

As soon as they stepped into the schoolhouse one of the teachers came up to them and ushered them to the coach's private office.

"Do you suppose he wants to see us about that deal last night?" Larry whispered as they stopped at the office door.

Danny Orlis nodded.

To their surprise, however, the whole football squad was crowded into the room.

"I've just told the rest of the squad about what happened last night, fellows," Coach Edwards said to Larry and Danny. "I wanted them to know why Eric is in trouble and why this game tomorrow night is the most important one we've ever played."

The players all nodded seriously. Now they just had to win that game!

Chapter 22

THE SEASON ENDS AT IRON MOUNTAIN

THAT EVENING when football practice was over Danny and Larry left the schoolhouse together and started toward town.

"Let's go and see Peggy and Eric," the young woodsman said as they approached the hospital.

"It's after visiting hours," Larry countered.

"But they each have a private room," Danny told him. "Maybe they even have private nurses. I think we can slip in for a couple of minutes."

They went into the hospital, but were not allowed to enter Eric's room. "He's not conscious," the nurse said, "and we cannot allow any visitors."

Peggy's nurse wasn't going to let them in to see her, either, but Peggy recognized Danny's voice. "I want to talk to Danny," she said weakly.

"Well, all right," the nurse agreed. "But only for a moment."

Danny and Larry stepped into the small white room and stood self-consciously by the bed. For a couple of minutes no one said a word. Peggy looked pale and weak, and every now and then her lip trembled uncertainly. Her forehead was bandaged and her arm was in a cast. The equipment for blood transfusions was still in the far corner of the room.

"How's Eric?" she asked at last, her voice almost a whisper.

"He's pretty sick," Danny told her. "They wouldn't let us see him."

"He's in trouble too, isn't he?" she persisted.

Danny nodded silently. He wished that he could tell her something else, but she had asked him, and he had to tell her the truth.

"What are they going to do to him, Danny?" she asked.

He shook his head.

"I—I've got to know." She took a pale white hand from under the sheet and laid it on his arm. "They're going to send him away, aren't they?"

"He hasn't had a trial yet," the young woodsman told her.

"I know they'll send him to the reformatory," she said, her voice trembling. "Won't they, Larry?"

"That was what Woody Blackburn was there for," Danny's cousin said reluctantly. "They gave him a year for it."

"Sheriff Riley told me that they intended to prosecute as hard as they could," Danny added.

"They want to set an example to keep other boys from doing the same thing."

The boys had thought that Peggy would burst into tears, and the nurse moved closer and was frowning her disapproval, but to their surprise Peggy was dry eyed.

"I prayed for Eric," she went on. "I prayed for him all the time, but it didn't do any good."

Danny and Larry were silent. What could they say?

"I'll never forget what you told me about being sure that my dates knew Christ as their Saviour," she added. "I knew you were right when you were telling me that, but I thought I just couldn't give Eric up. I had fooled myself into thinking that I could win him to Christ. I had made myself believe that was the real reason I kept going with him. And I did ask him to go to church and talked to him about the Lord a couple of times."

She stopped a moment and Danny pulled up a chair and sat down.

"The first thing I knew," she said, "he was leading me farther from the Lord all the time. Just think, if I'd followed your advice, Danny, I wouldn't be in a mess like this. And Eric wouldn't be lying in there so badly hurt. Believe me, from now on I'm not even going to have one date with a boy unless he's a Christian."

"I think that's the only safe way," Danny agreed.

The nurse came over then and asked the boys to leave.

Three days later the whole town was tingling with excitement. School let out at noon and there was a big pep rally in the auditorium. The mayor and a couple of former football players gave little talks and the football team was introduced to the people.

Danny and Larry heard that Eric had regained consciouness and when school was out went up to see him.

"What are you two doing here?" Eric snarled, bristling. "Squealers!"

Danny felt the color come up in his cheeks.

"Even my own lawyer says I'll get a year in the reformatory," Eric snapped. "And I owe that to you two!"

"We saw Peggy yesterday," Larry said, ignoring what the injured boy had said. "She's concerned about you."

"I'll bet she's concerned about me."

"You think everybody's down on you, Eric," Danny told him, trying to sound as understanding and concerned as possible. "But if you confess your sins and become a Christian you'll find that Jesus is one Friend who will never turn against you."

"You sound just like Peggy now!" Eric Tanner retorted. "Always preaching at me."

"Maybe it seems that way to you," the young woodsman said. "But it's only because we know what Jesus did for us and we want you to have the same thing."

Eric squirmed uncomfortably. "I'll become a Christian some day," he said. "When I get ready."

Danny took his Testament from his pocket and fingered it thoughtfully. "You know," he continued, "God may have spared you from being killed in that wreck so that you'd have one more chance to accept Christ as your Saviour."

"I'm not worried," Eric snorted. "I'll be okay." With that he turned over on his back and closed his eyes.

By game time Danny was so excited that he could scarcely tie his shoes.

"We've just got to win," Larry whispered to him as they ran out onto the field. "If we don't, people might get to thinking that we sold out the team, anyway."

Danny nodded grimly.

Spring Creek's squad was fully as strong as the sports writers had said it was, and the two squads seesawed back and forth across the field without scoring. Once or twice it looked as though the

Creek eleven was set up to punch a touchdown across, but the Iron Mountain line always rallied to hold at the last minute and take the ball on downs. It began to look as though the game would end without a score when Spring Creek tried a desperation pass in the dying moments of the final quarter and Larry intercepted it with a spectacular shoestring catch that brought the spectators howling to their feet.

The quarterback took a quick glance at the clock and called a play without taking the team into the huddle. Before the bewildered Spring Creek captain could regain his senses to call time out, the teams sprang into formation, the center snapped the ball, and Danny drifted back to pass.

Larry eluded the man who was guarding him and scampered into the flat in time to gather the bullet pass into his arms and dive across the goal line. The roar from the crowd drowned out the sound of the final gun!

Later, much later, when the boys finally had been photographed and interviewed and congratulated, they got into their street clothes and went home.

"Well," Danny said happily, "the season's over."

"And what a season it was!"

Danny sank into the nearest easy chair and took

a deep breath. "If Eric just wasn't in this trouble now," he said, "everything would be all right."

Larry nodded. "We've got to keep praying for him, Danny," he said fervently. "I don't know what would have happened to me if you hadn't kept on praying when I was in trouble."

"He'll come through for Christ," Danny said confidently. "I know he will!"